"Come with me, Penny. Outside."

"Are you crazy? It's after midnight, I'm in my nightgown and—"

The rest of the words tumbled back down Penny's throat when Jason picked her up off her feet. She wriggled and squirmed, hoping to make him set her down again. But he only tightened his grip on her and moved resolutely toward the back door.

"Put me down right now, Jason," Penny hissed. "Or I'll scream so loud everyone in this house will wake up."

"Is that really how you want our families to learn that you're carrying my child?"

Dear Reader,

Since the publication of my first Silhouette
Special Edition novel a little more than four years ago,
I've had the pleasure of working on four continuity
series. Each time, it's been a privilege to work with a
new group of authors, sharing story ideas, discussing
character motivations and brainstorming plot problems.
During the writing of this series, I also learned a lot of
interesting stuff about Texas, mining and jewelry design
(which was a *lot* of fun to research, although I had to
continually reassure my husband that I wasn't shopping
online—just writing☺).

Anyway, the result of all of this is *The Texas Tycoon's
Christmas Baby*. In this book, you'll get to know
Jason Foley and Penny McCord, you'll find out what
the other members of their families have been up to
since last month and you'll also catch a glimpse of
what the future may hold for all of them.

Happy reading and happy holidays!

Brenda Harlen

THE TEXAS TYCOON'S CHRISTMAS BABY

BRENDA HARLEN

SPECIAL EDITION

Published by Silhouette Books

America's Publisher of Contemporary Romance

Special thanks and acknowledgment to Brenda Harlen
for her contribution to
THE FOLEYS AND THE McCORDS miniseries.

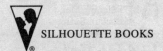

SILHOUETTE BOOKS

ISBN-13: 978-0-373-65498-7

THE TEXAS TYCOON'S CHRISTMAS BABY

Recycling programs
for this product may
not exist in your area.

Books by Brenda Harlen

BRENDA HARLEN

grew up in a small town surrounded by books and imaginary friends. Although she always dreamed of being a writer, she chose to follow a more traditional career path first. After two years of practicing as an attorney (including an appearance in front of the Supreme Court of Canada), she gave up her "real" job to be a mom and to try her hand at writing books. Three years, five manuscripts and another baby later, she sold her first book—an RWA Golden Heart Winner—to Silhouette Books.

Brenda lives in southern Ontario with her real-life husband/hero, two heroes-in-training and two neurotic dogs. She is still surrounded by books ("too many books," according to her children) and imaginary friends, but she also enjoys communicating with "real" people. Readers can contact Brenda by e-mail at brendaharlen@yahoo.com or by snail mail c/o Silhouette Books, 233 Broadway, Suite 1001, New York, NY 10279.

To the wonderful and talented Nicole Foster,
Crystal Green, Teresa Hill, Victoria Pade
and Karen Rose Smith—you proved to me that
writing doesn't have to be a solitary occupation.
Thanks for your help
and for making this project so much fun.

Thanks also to Susan Litman, for again thinking of me.

And to Charles Griemsman,
because it truly was a pleasure.

Prologue

Penny McCord was smiling when she hung up the phone after Jason Foley's call confirming their dinner plans. He was in Dallas on business and would stop by after his meetings finished to pick her up for a quiet, romantic evening at his condo. It would give her the perfect opportunity to share the news that had only been confirmed a few hours earlier, and then they could start planning their future together.

She was excited, of course, and just a little apprehensive. She wanted him to be as happy as she was, but as they had never talked about anything long-term, she couldn't be certain.

Still, she believed this was meant to be—fated, as was their meeting at Missy Harcourt's wedding only four short months ago. It was the only explanation she could think of for the fact that, in a room filled with more than five hundred guests, Jason Foley had noticed her.

When her own date for the occasion was called away, leaving Penny stranded, Jason had been there. He'd talked to her, danced with her, taken her home. And then he'd kissed her good night.

A few weeks later, they became lovers. She knew she was fortunate to have fallen in love with the man who'd been her first lover, and if Jason wasn't in love with her yet, she was hopeful it was only a matter of time before his feelings grew and deepened, as hers had done.

When the phone rang again, she assumed it was Jason calling her back—as he sometimes did—just to tell her he couldn't stop thinking about her.

"Miss me already?" she asked teasingly.

There was silence on the other end of the line and Penny mentally berated herself for not checking the call display before grabbing the receiver.

"Penny, it's Paige."

Her sister's voice sounded strained, as if she'd been crying. Not at all like her usual cheerful self.

"What is it? What's wrong?"

"Nothing. I just...I have to tell you something."

Aside from e-mail communications, they'd been out of touch for so long, and Penny had really missed talking to her twin. "I have some news, too, but it can wait. You go first."

But Paige didn't seem to be in any hurry, and as the silence lengthened, Penny's apprehension increased.

"Paige?" she prompted, wondering what could be so horrible that her sister couldn't seem to get the words out. Had she been in an accident? Was she ill? What was going on? "You're scaring me."

"I'm sorry, Penny. I'm so sorry about this. I love you. You know that, right? And I'll help you get through this, I promise."

Now she was even more confused. "Get through what?"

"Jason Foley."

She fell silent.

She and her twin had always been close, but it was only recently that Penny had told anyone she was dating Jason Foley. She didn't usually keep anything from her sister, but she'd justified her silence—at least to herself—on the basis that Paige was too preoccupied with her search for the Santa Magdalena Diamond to focus on anything else. But the truth was, Penny had worried that Paige wouldn't approve, that she would accuse her of being a fool for getting involved with anyone named Foley, and Penny refused to let an old feud get in the way of her relationship with the first man she'd ever loved.

"You have been seeing Jason Foley, right?" Paige asked her.

"Yes, I have," Penny said defiantly. "And I know that no one likes that, that no one understands. I can still hardly believe it myself, but he's not who you think he is, Paige. He's not who any of us thought he is. He's wonderful and sweet and kind, and I'm in love with him. And I think—" she mentally crossed her fingers, desperately hoping it was true "—he's in love with me, too."

"He's using you to get information about our family," Paige told her.

Penny was disappointed. Not in Jason, because she

didn't believe that Jason would do anything like that, but in her sister, for daring to accuse him of such deception.

She laughed to let her sister know that her relationship with Jason was solid and that she wouldn't let unfounded accusations undermine it. "No, he's not."

"Yes, he is," Paige insisted, and the quiet conviction in her voice gave Penny pause.

"He wouldn't do that," she said again. "He's not like that."

"I'm at Travis Foley's ranch right now, looking for the diamond. Travis was with me when I read Gabby's e-mail telling me you were seeing Jason, and Travis knew... He knew what his brother was going to do."

Penny wasn't sure which of her sister's revelations surprised her more. "No," she said, but with less certainty this time. She didn't want to listen to anything else Paige said about Jason. She knew there was a lot of bad history between the McCords and the Foleys, but she really believed Jason cared about her. How could he have said the things he'd said, done the things he'd done, if he didn't care about her?

Penny gnawed on her lip, considering what her sister had just told her. Jason hadn't made any mention of the infamous gem in the past several weeks, but she did recall earlier references, questions subtly slipped into a conversation that might have been intended to elicit information from Penny. Or maybe he'd just been making conversation. She wasn't going to assume the worst just because her sister had done so.

"That's crazy," she said.

"Honey, listen to me. I'm sorry, but Travis admitted the whole thing. Jason told Travis and their other brother, Zane, months ago what he was going to do. He was convinced our family was up to something to do with the diamond, and that the Foleys needed to know what that was. Jason thought he could get the information from you. By getting to know you. By pretending he was interested in you."

Penny didn't want to believe it, but…

"I'm so sorry. I could kill him with my bare hands, I swear. I will make him pay. We'll make all of them pay for what he did to you."

"I thought…" Penny could barely choke out the words now. "I thought I was in love with him."

I thought he loved me, too.

And now all of Penny's hopes and dreams for the future were shattered.

Chapter One

Jason Foley pulled into the long, winding drive that led to his brother's ranch and wondered what the heck he was doing out in the middle of nowhere when he had at least a dozen projects demanding his attention back at his office in Dallas. But Travis didn't ask for much, so Jason found it hard to refuse when his brother did make a request. And for some reason, it was important to his little brother to have the family all together for Thanksgiving this year. And not just to share the traditional meal, but the whole weekend.

Jason might not have minded even that so much except that, for some inexplicable reason, Travis had extended the invitation to include the McCord family, as well. It wasn't so many years ago that the Foleys and McCords would sooner have shot at each other than sat down at a table together, but apparently things had changed.

Unbidden, an image of Penny McCord's smiling face came to mind. Yeah, things had changed. And he felt a pang of loss. He still didn't know what had gone wrong between them, but after weeks of unreturned phone calls and ignored e-mails, he'd finally given up. Obviously, Penny had decided that she was finished with him, and that was fine. The only reason their relationship had lasted as long as it did was that Jason had felt guilty for his deception.

Truth be told, he still felt guilty. It had been his idea to get close to Penny McCord, to find out what she knew about her family's search for the Santa Magdalena Diamond. But it had been a plan born out of desperation, and not one that had sat well with him, even from the beginning.

As he'd grown closer to Penny, his guilt had grown along with his genuine affection for her. So when she stopped taking his calls, he'd almost been as relieved as he was baffled, because he knew that she was better off without him.

And he was better off without her. And if she did decide to show up at his brother's house for the holiday celebration, he would be polite and friendly while maintaining an emotional and physical distance. Maybe she'd meant something to him for a while, but that was over.

Or so he believed, until he walked into the kitchen and found her in his brother's arms.

"Well, isn't this a cozy little scene?"

The words were spoken through a jaw that was clenched as tightly as the fists that hung at Jason's sides.

Travis and Penny sprang apart—and it was then that

Jason saw through the haze of red that had clouded his vision to recognize his mistake.

It wasn't Penny in his brother's embrace, but her twin sister, Paige.

Of course it wasn't Penny. Even before he recognized her sister, he should have recognized that Penny wasn't the type of woman who would move quickly or easily from one man's bed to another's. In fact, she hadn't been in any man's bed until he'd taken her to his own.

And then she tossed him out of her life.

So why should he care if she'd picked up with someone else since then?

He shouldn't. But he did. And it was that realization which annoyed him more than anything else.

"I didn't mean to interrupt," he said now, his fingers slowly uncurling.

"You're early," Travis said, but the admonition was tempered by a smile that assured his brother he didn't really mind.

"I can leave and come back later."

"No need." Travis took Paige's hand and tugged her forward. "You know Paige McCord?"

Jason inclined his head. "It's good to see you again, Paige."

"I wish I could say the same," she responded coolly.

He looked at his brother, his brows lifted in silent inquiry. Travis gave a subtle shake of his head, but Jason wasn't prepared to let her remark pass without comment.

"If you're harboring some kind of grudge on behalf of your sister, you should know that she was the one who ended our relationship," he pointed out.

"And you don't have a clue why, do you?"

Even three weeks later, he didn't—a fact which continued to frustrate him.

"Can we not get into this now?" Travis asked, suggesting to Jason that he knew more than he'd shared with his brother.

"I'd like nothing more than to not get into this," Paige assured him. "In fact, I'd like nothing more than to pretend that your brother was never involved with my sister, but that's not possible now."

And with that, she tossed her hair over her shoulder and exited the room.

"Want to explain that to me?" Jason asked his brother.

Travis just shook his head again. "I'll leave that to Penny, if she's so inclined."

Jason's heart skipped a beat. "Then she is coming?"

"I told you I'd invited all of the McCords."

"But you didn't tell me Penny would be here."

"Would that information have affected your decision to come?"

"No," Jason said. "My decision had nothing to do with Penny McCord."

But even as he spoke the words, he knew that his brother didn't believe them any more than he did.

She shouldn't have come.

As Penny McCord sat wedged between Blake and Tate, her two older brothers, at the long table in Travis Foley's dining room, she wondered why she'd ever let herself be talked into making an appearance at this "family" dinner. Of course, she'd only accepted the invitation because she'd been certain that Travis's brother wouldn't.

Jason Foley was far too busy to take the time for a

long weekend at his brother's ranch. To his mind, business took precedence over family. In fact, business took precedence over everything else, and he would do anything to ensure the company's success. Their sham of a relationship was proof enough of that fact.

When the invitation to share in a Thanksgiving celebration had come through her sister, Penny was anxious to get away from the city, eager to spend some time with her twin, and desperate to cry on the shoulder that had always been there for her. So she'd gratefully said yes, certain that Jason would never take time away from his office to spend the holiday at his brother's isolated Texas ranch.

Apparently she'd been wrong.

Because every single member of the Foley family—Jason included—was in attendance, along with the entire McCord clan. As if the bitterness and animosity that had governed all McCord-Foley interactions of the past century was simply forgotten.

She knew the story—at least as it had been passed down through the McCord family. According to that history, the McCord and the Foley families of Texas had been feuding ever since Civil War, but the feud really heated up in the late 1890s, when Gavin Foley lost his claim to a West Texas silver mine to Harry McCord in a poker game. Gavin Foley swore the game was fixed and that Harry was a card cheat.

At the time, no one paid too much attention to the allegations and everyone thought the claim to be worthless. But there were rumors that the deed, which also served as the map to the mine, contained clues to the location of a buried treasure—including the legendary and supposedly cursed Santa Magdalena Diamond.

No treasure was ever found, though the disputed claim did turn out to be filled with silver ore, which is how the McCords acquired their family fortune. But rumors about the Santa Magdalena Diamond refused to die, especially after the recent discovery of a sunken ship in the Gulf of Mexico—the last known location of the infamous gem. The diamond wasn't on board, and since then, adventurers, gem collectors and jewel thieves from around the world had been searching for the legendary stone.

Penny wasn't sure she even believed that the Santa Magdalena Diamond existed; though, if it did, it was supposedly the world's largest, most perfect canary diamond, reputed to rival the Hope Diamond in beauty and size. But she *was* inclined to believe in the curse— the allegation that the gem had caused misfortune to everyone who had ever possessed it, including an Indian pasha, an Italian Renaissance prince, a seventeenth-century duke and an eighteenth-century Mexican governor—because, although she'd never even set eyes on the jewel, it seemed that her scant knowledge of its rumored existence had led directly to her heartache.

It could be argued that it was her own inexperience and naïveté that had caused her to fall for Jason Foley's seduction routine, and she knew there was some truth to that; but the fact remained that the COO of Foley Industries would never have looked twice in her direction if he wasn't interested in what she knew—or what he thought she knew—about the McCords' search for the diamond.

She determinedly pushed all thoughts of the gem and the Foley-McCord feud from her mind. She wasn't sure how much was fact and how much was fiction, and she didn't really care. She wasn't thinking of old grudges or ancient grievances now. No, her thoughts were on more recent events, more immediate hurts and personal heartaches. And being in the same room with Jason, so close and somehow so far away, scraped the scab off of a wound that had barely begun to heal.

It was the first time she'd seen him, face-to-face, since she'd learned that their entire relationship was a sham.

And the first time since she'd learned that she was going to have his baby.

A baby she had yet to tell him about, despite her sister's urging.

Paige kept telling Penny that Jason had a right to know that he was going to be a father, and Penny knew it was true. She also knew that Paige didn't just want her to share the news with her baby's father, she wanted to ensure that Jason was held responsible for his actions, which meant paying his share.

But Penny wasn't ready to deal with such practical matters. She was hurting too much to put the heartache aside and calmly discuss things like visitation and child support. Besides, she was doing well enough financially that she was confident she could support herself and her child—though the recent difficulties at McCord Jewelers did worry her enough that she tried not to think about them. Her job was as secure as anyone else's at the company, and not just because of her last name but because of the reputation she'd established for herself in the jewelry-design business.

Still, there was no way she was going to ask Jason Foley for anything. Not ever again.

She jolted when she felt an elbow in her ribs and frowned at her brother.

"Gabby asked you to pass the salad," Tate prompted.

"Oh. Sorry." She looked at the dishes on the table before realizing that she held the bowl of salad in her hand, then offered it to her cousin across the table. Glancing down at her plate, she saw that she hadn't taken any for herself. She had, however, put a lot of parmesan cheese on her pasta—and she didn't even like parmesan. She picked up her fork and pushed the noodles around on her plate.

Gabriella nudged Penny's foot under the table to get her attention. "Are you okay?" she whispered quietly.

Penny nodded, though she couldn't meet her cousin's gaze.

"Is it Jason?"

To her credit, Gabby didn't actually say the words aloud so much as she mouthed them across the table, but Penny cast a quick glance toward the man in question, who was seated immediately beside her cousin, and was relieved to find that he was in conversation with his young niece, seated on his other side. Still, the question obliterated any remaining hope that she and Jason had managed to keep their short-lived relationship a secret from anyone.

She shook her head.

But Gabriella obviously didn't believe her, because she leaned a little closer and said, "If you ever want to talk about—"

Penny shook her head again, more decisively this time. The absolute last thing she wanted was to talk about how Jason Foley had used her and how she'd been fool enough to let him, fool enough to believe that a man like him could ever seriously be interested in her.

She felt the sting of tears at the back of her eyes but furiously blinked them away.

Thankfully, Gabriella didn't have the chance to question her further, as Rafael leaned close to whisper something in his wife's ear, and whatever that something was, it brought a luminous smile to Gabby's face.

Penny looked away. That was the thing about national holidays and family gatherings—she was always surrounded by couples, and she was always alone.

This year seemed even worse, because the new faces around her weren't temporary ones that would be replaced next year, as had frequently happened in the past. Because somehow, in the space of six months, everyone around her had miraculously fallen in love.

Gabby and Rafael eloped after a whirlwind courtship, and though many had wondered about a match between the heiress and her bodyguard, it was obvious that they were madly in love with one another. Both of her older brothers were now affianced—and if her brother Tate's involvement with Tanya Kimbrough— daughter of the McCords' longtime housekeeper—had taken everyone aback, that surprise paled in comparison to Blake's engagement to Katie Whitcomb-Salgar, Tate's ex-girlfriend.

More recently, Penny's twin sister had hooked up with Travis Foley. And even her mother had partnered up— with Jason's father, of all people. Of course, Rex Foley was also the father of Penny's youngest brother, Charlie, which revelation had come as a shock to everyone, Charlie included. Apparently the Foley-McCord feud had come to an end twenty-two years earlier, at least so far as Eleanor and Rex were concerned.

The sound of a fork tapping against a wineglass drew Penny's attention back to the present and to Travis Foley at the end of the table. He waited until the various conversations had halted before addressing the group.

"Paige and I have some news that we wanted to share with you, news of something that we can all be thankful for this Thanksgiving."

Paige smiled, her eyes glowing with excitement as she faced the assembled guests. "We found the Santa Magdalena Diamond."

"The Santa Magdalena Diamond," Eleanor echoed, stunned. "All these years…I was never sure it was even real."

"It's real," Paige assured her. "And it's absolutely stunning."

An assessment that was confirmed by the gasps and sighs that sounded when Travis set the spectacular forty-eight-karat diamond on the table for everyone to see.

"I knew it was real," Blake McCord said. "And that it would be the answer to all of our problems, if only we could find it."

"And you knew that it was probably hidden somewhere in the abandoned mines on this land."

"If that's where you found it—on McCord property—then the diamond is rightfully ours," the McCord CEO asserted.

"But Travis is the rightful lessee of the property," Jason interjected. "So the diamond is his."

"Paige and I found it together, so the diamond is ours," Travis said, in a tone that brooked no argument.

"And after much discussion," Paige continued, "we've

decided to donate it—and the chest of ancient silver coins we found along with it—to the Smithsonian."

"But—" Blake began, only to snap his mouth shut in response to the look he got from his sister.

"Of course, we're going to take advantage of all the publicity we can get from the discovery," Paige continued. "And although we've notified the Smithsonian of the find and our intention to donate the stone, we're going to display the diamond at our flagship store in Dallas for a few months prior to making the donation official."

"That will certainly generate traffic to the store," Gabby said approvingly.

"And increase revenues for the business," Rafael affirmed.

"A brilliant PR move," Tate decided.

"Thanks," Paige said dryly.

"I'd hoped the McCords would benefit exclusively from the treasure," Blake unexpectedly admitted to the assembled guests. "But since it's obvious that my sister Paige, found love during her search, an even greater treasure than the Santa Magdalena Diamond…" his gaze drifted from the gem to his fiancée "…I can't say that I'm at all disappointed to have to share the discovery."

"We found something else, too," Paige interjected, smiling at Travis.

"What more could there be?" Tanya wondered aloud, causing laughter to ripple around the table.

"McCordite," Paige said, which announcement elicited various expressions of confusion.

"What's that?" Charlie finally asked.

"This." She set a chunk of another type of rock down on the table beside the diamond.

It wasn't quite as big or as brilliant as the Santa Magdalena Diamond, of course, but it was pretty spectacular in its own right. And, even more impressive, it seemed to change color depending on the angle of the light. From the softest pink to the palest blue to shimmering gold, the gem's smooth, flawless surface seemed to reflect the hopes and dreams of anyone who gazed upon it.

"But what is it?" Charlie asked again.

"That's what Travis and I have been trying to figure out, and after all of our research, what we know is that it is a previously undiscovered gem that seems to be unique to this part of the world. Which is why we're going to trademark it as 'McCordite'—and the mine is filled with it."

"A previously undiscovered gem must be worth a fortune," Blake noted.

"Always thinking of the bottom line," Katie teased her fiancé.

"Someone has to," he retorted, just a little defensively.

"And this will greatly improve our bottom line," Paige assured them all. "After Blake introduces it at the upcoming Tucson Gem Show."

"I'll be happy to," Blake promised.

"Before we move on to dessert," Travis said, his words silencing the renewed murmurs. "I have a request of Penny."

She set down the water glass she'd just picked up, suddenly aware that all eyes were focused in her direction, as she wondered what Jason's brother could possibly want from her.

"I'd like you to design an engagement ring to showcase the new gem," he told her. "Because I've asked Paige to marry me—and she said 'yes'."

Penny swallowed around the lump in her throat and forced her lips to curve into a semblance of a smile. She was happy for her sister—she really was. She just couldn't help but wish that her own relationship hadn't ended so unhappily. "It would be my pleasure."

Suddenly everyone was talking again, offering congratulations and toasts to the newly engaged couple.

And even while Penny's mind was already working through materials and designs for her sister's engagement ring, she felt a pang inside of her chest. She was thrilled for her sister, of course, but in the midst of so many happy couples, she couldn't help wishing that she'd found something more than heartache.

"To the future bride and groom," Melanie, Zane's former nanny, now girlfriend, said.

Travis and Paige both drank from their glasses, then they kissed.

Penny tore her gaze away from the intimacy—and found Jason's gaze locked on her.

Jason had been watching Penny all night, unable to tear his eyes away, subconsciously urging her to glance in his direction. He wanted just one moment of eye contact, certain that one quick look would confirm that the connection they'd shared had fizzled, convinced that was all he needed to be able to put her out of his mind and get on with his life without her.

What he saw in her eyes was surprise and hurt and yearning.

And what he felt was heat that seared all the way to his toes.

The connection had definitely *not* fizzled.

But something had gone wrong, and he needed to know what it was if he had any hope of fixing it.

He let his eyes skim over her face, as if he hadn't memorized every detail during the time they'd spent together. But there were subtle changes since he'd seen her last. Her cheekbones were a little more prominent, her skin a little too pale, and there were dark smudges under her eyes that suggested she hadn't slept any better than he had in the weeks they'd been apart. But most notable—and most damning—were the shadows that lingered in the depths of her beautiful green eyes.

She tore her gaze away, and the all-too-brief moment was lost, leaving Jason with the surreal feeling that she'd somehow reached inside of him and wrenched his heart right out of his chest.

And in that moment, he realized that it was an entirely appropriate analogy, because she did have his heart. Or at least more of it than he'd ever given to any other woman in a very long time.

He'd had a lot of relationships in his thirty-two years. Too many relationships with too many women who never really mattered to him. In fact, since the tragic end of his relationship with Kara, his college girlfriend, he couldn't think of any woman who had mattered…until Penny.

When she'd called and left a message on his voice-mail, canceling their last scheduled date, he'd been more surprised than anything. When she stopped answering his calls and failed to respond to any of his messages, he'd grown concerned. But his worry quickly gave way to annoyance when he realized that she was still going about her usual routine and had simply cut him out of the picture.

He'd tried to convince himself that their break-up was inevitable, that he never intended for it to be long-term. In fact, he'd never really intended to get involved with her at all, not beyond some casual dating and simple flirting to get the information he wanted about her family's search for the legendary Santa Magdalena Diamond.

Yes, it had all started because of the diamond, because his brother had overheard some talk at a party and become convinced that the McCords were in search of the fabled gem. And because Jason had been determined to discover what they knew, to learn how close they were to finding the long-lost treasure.

Then he'd started spending time with Penny, getting to know her, and he'd forgotten that he had an agenda. When he was with Penny, she somehow managed to make him forget about everything but the pleasure of being with her.

His gaze shifted to the diamond at the center of the table, the stunning gem taunting him with the knowledge that what he'd once sought so desperately now meant nothing in comparison to what he'd so briefly had—and lost.

He glanced at Penny again, but she wasn't looking in his direction. She'd been deliberately *not* looking in his direction since she sat down across from him at the table, as if by refusing to acknowledge his presence she could pretend he wasn't there.

She'd been doing that for weeks now, acting as if she didn't know him, as if they'd never meant anything to one another. Now that the fires of the ancient Foley-McCord feud had finally been banked, he didn't want to be the one to add fuel, but he also wasn't going to let Penny's campaign of avoidance continue.

He wasn't going to be ignored any longer.

Chapter Two

Penny stayed at the table only until dessert had been served, then she picked up her dishes and pushed her chair back. She wasn't particularly fond of kitchen duty, but at the moment, it was infinitely preferable to enduring another minute of Jason's scrutiny.

How could he look at her like that? As if he cared. As if he still wanted her, when he'd never really wanted her in the first place.

She exhaled a weary sigh as she scraped the remnants of her dinner into the garbage can and considered how rude it would be to leave the ranch now, without telling anyone.

Inexcusably rude, her conscience—sounding a great deal like her no-nonsense sister—warned.

She sighed again, because she knew it was true.

"Something weighing on your mind?" an achingly familiar voice asked from behind her.

Penny whirled around, and found herself face-to-face with Jason.

Her breath caught in her throat, her heart hammered against her ribs and her knees went as limp as the uneaten spaghetti she'd just dumped. She set her bowl down and gripped the edge of the counter for support. "What are you doing here?"

"I wanted to see you."

"Well, I don't want to see you."

"So you've said to my answering machine and on my voice mail and to my secretary, but you've never said it to me."

"I just did."

"But not without that little catch in your voice that leads me to believe the words aren't really true."

"Go away, Jason."

"I tried," he admitted. "But I can't get you out of my mind."

"The game is over, Jason. Travis and Paige found the Santa Magdalena Diamond—there's no reason to pretend you really care about me anymore."

"You think I was pretending?"

"I *know* you were pretending. I know that from our first dance at Missy Harcourt's wedding to the last night I spent in your bed, it was all about the diamond."

"Everything okay in here?" Gabriella asked, carrying an armful of dishes into the kitchen.

"Fine," Penny said, although her cheeks flamed at the realization that her cousin couldn't have failed to overhear the words she'd spoken.

"Actually," Jason said, "Penny and I would like a few minutes alone, if you don't mind."

Gabby looked at her cousin, as if for confirmation.

Penny refused to give it. "No, we don't."

She knew she was going to have to talk to Jason, that they were going to have to find a way to communicate and make plans for their baby, but not yet. Not when simply being in the same room with him made her heart ache.

"Please, Penny," Jason said.

And her aching heart melted, just a little.

But before she could respond to his plea, Paige came to her rescue. She sailed into the kitchen and, summing up the situation in one quick glance, turned to Jason and said, "Out."

Though Gabby had to know that her cousin wasn't talking to her, she slipped out of the room, obviously not wanting to get caught in any cross fire.

Jason's brows lifted. "I'm simply trying to help with the cleanup."

Paige's smile was forced. "You've done enough. Really."

Penny knew her sister was referring to his relationship with her, rather than the state of the kitchen, and, judging by the way his eyes narrowed, Jason knew it, too.

"I'll catch up with you later," he said to Penny.

She nodded, accepting that it was inevitable, even while she hoped it would be *much* later.

"I can't believe that man is Travis's brother," Paige muttered.

"Which means he's soon going to be your brother-in-law," Penny pointed out. "So maybe you should try being a little less hostile toward him."

"I'm only looking out for you."

"I know. And I appreciate it. But I need to stand on my own two feet."

"Not an easy task when you've had the rug pulled right out from under you."

"I can manage," she assured her sister.

"Manage the dishes all by yourself?" Gabby teased, returning to the kitchen. "Because I'd much rather linger over another glass of wine than tackle the logistical nightmare of loading fourteen place settings into a dishwasher."

"Then you're in luck," Penny said, squirting soap into the stream of hot water that was rapidly filling one of the sinks. "You can scrub the pots instead."

To the sisters' mutual surprise, Gabby didn't balk at the directive, but moved to the sink and immersed her hands into the sudsy water.

"I wish I had a camera," Paige murmured, heading back out to the dining room to finish clearing the tables.

"I know I've been spoiled and pampered most of my life," Gabby said. "But Rafael has been encouraging me to overcome my aversion to domestic chores."

"Still—" Penny handed her cousin a pair of rubber gloves "—the McCord spokesperson can't be caught with dishpan hands."

"Speaking of hands," Gabby said, drying her own in order to don the gloves as Paige returned. "Did either of you notice, when Eleanor and Rex lifted their glasses to toast the new engagement, that they both had gold bands on the third fingers of their left hands?"

"I didn't," Penny admitted, frowning.

She hadn't really been able to concentrate on anything with Jason so near, and she couldn't help but wonder how wrapped up in him she'd been over the past few months, that she'd been so oblivious to the developing relationship between her mother and his father.

"Neither did I," Paige said, then, "Are you sure?"

"Positive."

"Are you actually suggesting that our mother got married without telling her kids?"

Gabby shrugged. "Well, everyone's been so caught up in their own lives and their own agendas lately, and with the volatile history between the two families, she probably just wanted to do it quietly."

It made sense, sort of. "But why didn't they tell us today?"

"Maybe they intended to," Gabby suggested. "But didn't want to steal the spotlight from the news that Paige is engaged to her stepbrother."

"Well, good for Mom, I guess, though the stepbrother thing is a little disconcerting."

"Talk about close family ties," Gabby mused.

"A little too close," Penny said.

"And don't think the media won't figure out the connection," their cousin warned.

A former model, international jetsetter and genuine blueblood heiress, Gabriella had been the target of more than her fair share of media attention and was understandably wary.

Paige just shrugged. "At this point, any publicity for the family is good for the business."

"Even a headline that reads: 'Family Feud Ends with Stepsibling Wedding'?" Gabby asked, determined to ensure that her cousin understood the kind of paparazzi circus she might find herself in the midst of.

"It's better than 'McCord Heiress Gives Birth to Stepbrother's Illegitimate Baby'."

Gabby stared at Paige. "You're pregnant?"

In response to which question Paige automatically shook her head, then winced when she realized the truth that her denial revealed.

Gabby spun around to face Penny.

Penny didn't—couldn't—respond. Nor could she hide the tears that sprang to her eyes.

"Good thing I swore you to secrecy on that," she said to her sister.

Paige winced again. "Oh, honey, I wasn't thinking."

"Apparently, neither was I, or I wouldn't be in this mess."

"Does Jason know?" Gabby asked gently.

"Not unless he was lurking outside the doorway when Paige made her little announcement."

"But you're going to tell him?" her cousin pressed. "Because he seems to me like the type of guy who would step up to do the right thing."

"What is the right thing in this situation?" Penny wondered aloud.

"To get married and give your baby a family."

She shook her head, her throat tight. It was once what she'd wanted, more than anything else. When she'd first learned that she was carrying Jason's baby, she'd foolishly let herself imagine that he would be thrilled by the news, that he would want to marry her and be a father to their child. Then she'd found out that their entire relationship had been a scam from the beginning, and her dream had shattered.

* * *

Maybe it had been a mistake to come.

Jason considered this possibility as he made his way down the hall.

It had definitely been a mistake to think that he could resolve anything with Penny while there were so many other people around, one of whom was her overprotective twin sister. But it was the first opportunity he'd had to see her and talk to her face-to-face since she canceled their dinner plans and stopped taking his calls almost three weeks earlier, and he'd prematurely jumped at the opportunity. And blown it.

Frustrated with himself as much as the situation, he pushed open the door and stepped out onto the porch, nearly tripping over Olivia, his six-year-old niece, in the process. His oldest brother, Livie's father, was waiting for her at the bottom of the stairs.

"Where are you rushing off to?" Zane asked him.

"I was just coming out to get some air," Jason replied.

"We're going to see the kittens," Olivia announced.

"Kittens?"

She nodded enthusiastically. "Uncle Travis said Matilda had a letter of six."

"A litter," Zane corrected his daughter.

"Six kittens," Olivia said, refocusing her attention on the most important piece of information. "They're in the barn."

"Then we should definitely go take a look," Jason agreed, and his response was rewarded with a brilliant smile from his niece.

Olivia skipped ahead. Zane and Jason followed at a more leisurely pace, a few steps behind.

"Good thing it's a clear night," Zane noted. "Living in the city, I forget how dark it can get out here."

"I don't know that I could ever live out in the middle of nowhere, but it seems to suit Travis."

"Hopefully, it will suit Paige, too."

Jason nodded.

"It's kind of funny how things work out, isn't it? I mean, Paige came out here to basically steal the diamond from under our brother's nose, and somehow they ended up falling in love."

"Funny? Seems like falling in love has become an epidemic."

Zane chuckled. "Don't knock it till you try it."

"Thanks, but I'll pass."

"In that case, you must be pleased that Travis and Paige found the diamond."

"What does that have to do with anything?"

"Well, it gets you off the hook, so far as things with Penny McCord are concerned."

"Yeah, it does that," Jason said, with a decided lack of enthusiasm.

"Imagine how awkward it would be for everyone if Eleanor found out you were dating her daughter to get information about the McCords' search for the diamond. Especially now that our father seems to have hooked up with her mother."

"What do you mean—Dad has hooked up with Eleanor?"

Zane stared at him. "You didn't notice that they arrived together?"

Jason shook his head. "I thought they just happened to show up at the same time."

"Did you see the two of them at dinner?"

He shook his head again.

"They could hardly take their eyes off of one another. And they were the first to leave after the meal, as if they couldn't wait to be alone together."

"Please—" Jason held up a hand, halting any further explanation "—there are some things I don't need to know."

"It's funny, isn't it? They apparently fell in love when they were teenagers, but went their separate ways, and have now rediscovered one another so many years later."

"Apparently they rediscovered one another quite a few years ago," Jason said, a not-so-veiled reference to the existence of Charlie McCord, Eleanor's youngest son, who was recently revealed to be their half-brother, the result of a brief affair she had with their father during a period of separation from her husband.

"Still, it's good to see him happy again. To know that he has someone to spend his life with, that he's not alone anymore."

"If that's what makes him happy," Jason agreed.

"Come on," Olivia said impatiently, already at the door of the barn.

"We're coming," her father assured her.

Satisfied with that response, she disappeared inside the building.

"What's it going to take to make you happy?" Zane asked.

Jason followed his brother into the barn. "I am happy."

"Yeah, that's why you've practically been living at the office over the past couple of weeks."

"There's been a lot going on at Foley Industries. Big deals that need a lot of work and personal attention from the COO."

"Is that really it?" his brother pressed. "Or is it that you have no one to go home to?"

"I never wanted anyone to go home to," he said, keeping his voice low, in the hope that his niece wouldn't overhear.

"You should have a kitten," Olivia decided, proving that she had excellent hearing. "That would be someone to go home to."

Jason managed a smile. "A kitten would be very lonely at my apartment, because I'm not there very much."

"Maybe you could take the kitten to work with you."

"She doesn't give up, does she?" Jason asked his brother.

"Never," Zane agreed. "I must have told her a thousand times that we aren't going to take one of Travis's kittens home with us, yet here we are, and you can bet she's already picked out the one she wants."

"There was a time when I knew what I wanted, too," Jason admitted.

"And now?"

"I don't seem to have a clue."

"I think you do," Zane told him. "I think you know exactly what you want—or maybe it would be more appropriate to say *who* you want."

Jason couldn't deny it. "I screwed up, Zane."

"I never really approved of your plan to get close to Penny McCord in order to get information about the Santa Magdalena Diamond—"

"Yes, you made that abundantly clear."

"—but despite that," Zane continued, as if Jason hadn't spoken, "I think the time you spent with her was good for you. I think she was good for you."

Jason couldn't deny that assessment, either. Penny had been good for him, but he hadn't returned the favor. He'd lied to her and used her, and she had every right to be furious with him. Now the only question that remained in his mind was: did he have any right to try to fix things, or should he just let her go?

Penny followed her sister up to the second floor. "Are you sure it's okay that I'm staying here? Because I could get a room at the hotel where the others are staying."

"Of course it's okay. The whole point of you coming for the weekend was so that we could spend some time together."

"I'd think you'd be more anxious to spend the time with your new fiancé." She opened the duffel bag that Travis had earlier taken up to the bedroom for her, and pulled out her nightgown.

"I would rather sleep with him than with you," Paige admitted with a smile. "But that would mean you sharing a room with Jason, which neither of us thought was a good idea, all things considered."

"Thank you for that."

"Although I'm starting to think that we might have been wrong. If you were sharing a room, you'd have the perfect opportunity to tell him about the baby."

"I will tell Jason about the baby," Penny agreed. "When I'm ready, not when you think I should be."

"When will that be?"

"Not now. Not here," Penny said.

"Why not?"

"Because I'm not ready."

"You can't keep your pregnancy a secret forever," her sister pointed out logically.

"I don't want to keep it a secret forever."

"Just for the next seven and a half months?" Paige guessed.

"Why are you so anxious for me to tell him?" Penny countered. "He never even wanted me—what makes you think he'll want this baby?"

"Actually, I might have been wrong about that."

Penny tugged her nightgown over her head. "Wrong about what?"

"That Jason was only using you to get information about the Santa Magdalena Diamond."

Penny stared at her sister.

"He was definitely using you," Paige hastened to explain. "Which still makes him scum of the earth, as far as I'm concerned. But the way he was looking at you all through dinner makes me suspect that his feelings for you might not have been entirely manufactured."

"That possibility makes me feel so much better," Penny said dryly.

"I'm not about to join the Jason Foley fan club," her sister assured her. "But I do believe in admitting when I'm wrong, and it's possible that I was wrong about him."

"It's also possible that your relationship with his brother has clouded your judgment with respect to other members of the family."

"My loyalty is—and will always be—to you."

"You're going to marry Travis Foley."

"You're still going to be my sister."

Penny had to look away, so Paige wouldn't see the tears that had filled her eyes.

Everything was changing—her sister had been lucky enough to find a man she could love and who loved her back. Penny was happy for her—and all too aware that she, too, was embarking on a new phase of her life, but that she would do so alone.

"If he never wanted you, he really is an idiot," Paige said loyally. "But he will want this baby, because it's his child—his heir to the Foley empire."

Her sister's warning lingered in her mind long after they turned out the lights. And though Penny was emotionally and physically exhausted, sleep continued to elude her, the words echoing in her head.

Or maybe it was the rumbling of her tummy that was keeping her awake.

She'd found it difficult to concentrate on the meal with Jason at the same dinner table, and almost impossible to force food into her churning stomach. That same stomach was sounding its protest now.

Penny glanced at the glowing numbers on the alarm clock: 11:47 p.m. Could she hold out until the morning? But if she did, chances were she'd be sitting at a table with Jason again, and not manage to eat anything.

With a silent oath, she pushed back the covers and headed out into the hall.

She hadn't packed a robe, but the quiet house assured her that everyone else was settled in for the night. The growling in her stomach seemed to intensify as she padded down the stairs. The second one from the bottom creaked when she stepped on it, but the rest of the house remained silent, except for the peanut butter sandwich calling her name.

Upstairs, in the guest room that he was sharing with Travis, because his brother had given up the master bedroom to his fiancée, it wasn't silent, though Jason was careful to keep his voice pitched low so as not to disturb the other guests.

"It all makes sense now," Jason said.

"What makes sense?" Travis had long ago settled on the narrow twin bed, on the opposite side of the room from the one his brother had claimed, and was flipping through channels on the television with the remote control.

"Why Penny doesn't even want to talk to me anymore." Jason paced the length of the room. "It was because of you. You told Paige about my plan to get information from Penny and she told her sister."

"I couldn't lie to her." Travis kept his eyes on the television, evading his brother's.

"Did you tell her that you were in agreement with the plan?" Jason challenged.

"The plan was to get information from her," Travis reminded him. "No one told you to seduce her."

"Maybe she seduced me."

His brother snorted his disbelief. "Regardless of who seduced whom—you slept with her, and that wasn't part of the plan."

"Nothing of what happened with Penny was part of the plan," he admitted.

Travis stopped scrolling through channels on the television, to give his brother his full attention. "Then you really do have feelings for her?"

"Why does that seem so unbelievable to you?"

"Because you made it clear from the beginning that your only purpose in getting close to Penny was to best the McCords."

"That was almost five months ago."

"Well, if your reasons for being with Penny changed, you might have let the rest of us in on it," Travis told him.

Which was a valid point, if not one that Jason was in the mood to acknowledge. Because although his reasons for being with Penny had changed, it wasn't something he'd been willing to admit to himself, never mind share with anyone else. So all he said was, "It was none of your damned business."

"But it was," Travis reminded him. "It was Foley business."

"No, it wasn't. What was between Penny and me wasn't business at all," Jason said, and, finally realizing it was true, stormed out of the room.

He resisted the urge to slam the door on his way out. Although the solid smack of wood against wood might be a satisfying reflection of the anger and frustration that were churning inside of him, he was conscious of the fact that his brother's house was filled with guests. The last thing he wanted were witnesses to his suddenly churning emotions, especially when two of those potential witnesses were sisters who were already ticked off at him enough without his temper interrupting their slumber.

So instead of slamming the door, he decided to take a walk, get some air and try not to think about how thoroughly he had destroyed any chance of a relationship with the most amazing woman he'd ever known.

He was on his way down the hall when he heard a

sound from the kitchen and, pausing at the doorway to investigate, found Penny at the counter.

She had her back to him, but this time there was no doubt in his mind as to which twin was standing in his brother's kitchen. The pain that stabbed through his heart and the need that twisted in his belly were proof enough of the fact.

She was wearing a long white nightdress that covered her from throat to ankles. Flannel, he guessed, as the heavy fabric didn't even give a hint of the luscious curves hidden beneath. But he knew the curves were there, he knew how soft her skin was, and he knew how she would quiver in response to his touch.

His hands itched with the need to reach out to her, but he curled them into fists.

"Penny."

She turned so quickly she swayed on her feet, nearly losing her balance.

He instinctively moved forward, reaching out to her.

She knocked his hand away, instead grabbing hold of the edge of the countertop to steady herself.

But she was pale. Too pale. The dark smudges under her eyes seemed even darker now, and he wondered if she was even half as lonely as he'd been since she ended their relationship.

"Are you all right?"

"I'm fine."

"You don't look fine," he said, and felt a twinge of guilt that he might in some way be responsible for that.

"I'm hungry," she said, and picked up half of the peanut butter sandwich she'd just cut.

"You didn't eat much dinner," he noted.

"I wasn't very hungry then."

"You didn't drink your wine, either."

"I wasn't thirsty." But she went to the fridge and poured herself a glass of milk now.

He remembered that her favorite late-night snack was a peanut butter sandwich, and that she always washed it down with a glass of milk. He'd never been particularly fond of peanut butter—until he tasted it on Penny's lips.

"You have every right to be upset with me," he said.

"Yes, I do." she agreed, but she sounded more weary than angry. "But not everything is about you, Jason."

He wanted to make her smile—to see her lips curve and watch some of the clouds lift from her eyes—so he tried to lighten the moment by asking, "Then you didn't skip the wine because you were afraid you wouldn't be able to control yourself around me?"

"No," she said, and looked him straight in the eye. "I skipped the wine because I'm pregnant."

Chapter Three

Penny had imagined a dozen scenarios in which she finally told Jason that she was going to have his child—but blurting out the news in his brother's kitchen wasn't one of them. And it never would have happened that way, except for Paige's nagging and the fact that she couldn't get the pregnancy out of her mind.

"Pregnant?" Jason echoed, confusion—and more than a hint of panic—evident in his deep blue eyes.

"Yes, Jason, I'm going to have a baby."

He swallowed. "You mean, you're going to have *my* baby."

"Yes," she said again.

He leaned back against the counter. "But we were careful."

"Not careful enough, obviously." And she knew that was her fault.

"Are you sure?"

"I took three different home pregnancy tests, and a couple of weeks ago, my doctor confirmed the results." Penny picked up the second half of her sandwich and nibbled. She wasn't feeling very hungry anymore, but she knew that she needed to eat, at least for the baby's sake.

"Come with me."

"What? Where?"

"Outside."

She dropped the rest of her sandwich back onto the plate. "Are you crazy? It's after midnight, I'm in my nightgown, and—"

The rest of the words tumbled back down her throat when Jason picked her up off her feet.

Obviously, he wasn't in a mood to debate the issue any more than she was in a mood to acquiesce to his demands. She wriggled and squirmed, hoping to make him set her down again. But he only tightened his grip on her and moved resolutely toward the back door.

"Put me down right now," she hissed. "Or I'll scream so loud everyone in this house will wake up."

"Is that really how you want our families to learn that you're carrying my child?"

She clamped her lips shut.

"Good answer," he said. "Although you might want to stop wriggling around so much, or I'm going to forget that I'm supposed to be too pissed off to get turned on."

She stopped wriggling. "Why are *you* pissed off at *me?*"

"No one's in the guest cottage," he said, ignoring her question. "We can talk there in private, without anyone else overhearing or interfering with our conversation."

He snagged a key off of a hook by the back door before he pushed it open and stepped out into the darkness.

She shivered as the cold night air hit, and he tightened his arms around her. "You might have just suggested that in the first place—"

"As if you would have meekly followed," he muttered.

"—instead of hauling me off the ground like a bag of laundry," she continued indignantly.

"Honey, no bag of laundry ever felt or smelled as good as you."

"Don't call me 'honey'," she snapped.

"You never objected to it before."

"I didn't object to a lot of things—because I didn't know that I was being played like a pawn in a chess game."

"It wasn't like that."

"Then you didn't get close to me for the sole purpose of finding out what I knew about the search for the Santa Magdalena Diamond?"

She wanted him to deny it, to insist that he cared about her, but his silence said otherwise. And when he finally set her on her feet to insert the key into the lock of the guest cottage, she was tempted to turn on her heel and march back to the main house. But that would be both petty and pointless, as he would only follow her again. And if he was determined to get answers to his questions, well, she had some questions of her own.

He reached inside to flick on the lights, then held open the door for her to enter. She did, and gasped when her bare feet came into contact with the cold, ceramic tile floor.

"I'll light a fire," Jason said, moving toward the stone fireplace on the far side of the room. "It will heat the cabin up quickly."

"Don't bother." Penny sat on the sofa, tucked her feet beneath her. "I don't plan on being here long enough for it to matter."

But once again Jason ignored her. He selected wood and kindling from the box on the hearth and, within minutes, there were flames crackling and blazing.

"How far along are you?"

She shrugged. "Almost fourteen weeks." She folded her arms across her chest. "Do you want a paternity test?"

He scowled at her. "Of course I don't want a paternity test."

She pushed off of the sofa, drawn to the heat of the fire. "You're a wealthy man—I'd be surprised if your lawyer didn't insist on it."

"Do you think maybe we could talk about this without bringing lawyers into it?"

"No matter how much talking we do, if you want to be a part of my baby's life, formal arrangements will have to be made."

"I'd rather see a minister than a lawyer."

It took her a minute to figure out what he was saying and, when she finally did, she couldn't help but laugh. "You're not seriously suggesting marriage?"

He frowned. "Why not?"

"Because we don't even like one another."

"I'd say the baby you're carrying proves otherwise."

"Maybe there was an attraction, for a while," she allowed.

But there was never any real affection. At least not on his part, and that was what—even now—hurt most of all.

"The attraction's still there," he insisted.

Penny shook her head. "Your family must be really

proud of you—to realize the extent to which you were willing to go to get the information you wanted."

"It wasn't supposed to go as far as it did."

"That makes me feel so much better," she said bitterly. "I didn't even make you work for it, did I? I was so willing, so pathetically eager to fall into bed with you."

"You were passionate." He turned her around so that she was facing him. "Incredibly passionate and wonderfully uninhibited."

"Fancy words for *'easy'*." She pulled away from him, moved back to the sofa, partly to give herself some space and partly because she was simply too tired to continue to stand. "Except you never really got what you wanted, did you? I couldn't tell you what you wanted to know because I didn't even know what Paige and Blake were doing. And I'll bet that annoys the hell out of you."

"But I did get what I wanted," he insisted. "Because the more time I spent with you, the less I cared about the damned diamond, the more I wanted you."

As if she was going to believe that now, after he'd dropped out of her life so quickly and completely.

Yeah, she was the one who stopped taking his calls. But if there was one thing she knew about Jason Foley after all the time they'd spent together, it was that he didn't give up on something he wanted. The fact that he gave up on her, and so easily, was just further proof that he'd never really wanted her.

"When I decided to try to get information from you, I didn't know you. I only knew that you were a McCord, and that seemed justification enough for what I was doing."

She didn't manage to hold back the yawn as she

watched him pace and listened to him talk. Now that she'd eaten, even if it was only half of a sandwich, she could no longer fight the exhaustion that had plagued her of late. Or maybe it hadn't been hunger that had been keeping her awake, but worry about how and when she was going to tell Jason about their baby.

Now that hurdle had been knocked down, and she felt her eyes drift shut.

"But as we spent more time together, as I got to know you better, I realized…"

Jason didn't think he'd ever been so open about his thoughts and his feelings, but never had there been so much at stake. He'd hurt Penny with his deception, and while he might have easily dismissed the possibility of such collateral damage as insignificant when he'd begun his campaign, she had become the most significant part of the campaign. And while he might have been willing to let her go, to protect himself from getting too deeply involved, now there was a baby to consider. He didn't really expect that she'd forgive him, but he wanted—no, he *needed*—to convince her to put it behind them so that they could move forward. Together.

He turned back, to gauge her reaction, to hear her response. And realized that none would be immediately forthcoming. Because somewhere along the line, while he'd been pouring out his heart and soul, Penny had fallen asleep.

He stared at her, stunned. He started across the room, determined to wake her so that they could finish their conversation. They were never going to resolve anything if they didn't talk about it.

But his steps faltered as he drew nearer.

She looked so fragile lying there. So pale and beautiful. The flannel gown she wore emphasized the slenderness of her frame. There was no evidence yet of the baby that was growing inside of her. His baby, he amended, and felt a quick spurt of something that might have been excitement or terror.

He definitely hadn't planned for this, wasn't ready for this. It was just another one of those strange curves that fate seemed to enjoy tossing at him, but he would step up to the plate. He *wanted* to step up to the plate. Maybe his mind was still reeling at the revelation of Penny's pregnancy, but he already knew that he wanted the baby. And he wanted his baby's mother.

He lifted her carefully from the sofa. She snuggled into him, her head pillowed against his shoulder. She wasn't protesting now—of course, that was only because she was sleeping, but he couldn't help but cherish the moment. It seemed so long since he'd held her in his arms, and he missed her.

Unable to resist, he dipped his head and dropped a gentle kiss on the side of her mouth. To his surprise, she tilted her head, her lips instinctively seeking—and finding—his. And though he knew he was taking advantage of her sleepy state, he couldn't resist her avid response.

Somehow, her arms found their way around his neck, and she pulled his head down, deepening the kiss. He tasted a hint of peanut butter, and the sweeter, much more seductive flavor that was uniquely her own.

Though she weighed next to nothing, he felt his arms tremble, and he knew it was his hunger for her that made him weak. And instead of carrying her to the door, as he'd intended, he carried her to the neatly made double bed.

He laid her gently on top of the spread, and she pulled him down with her, their mouths still fused together.

Guilt and worry tugged at his conscience, but her hands were on him, sliding up his chest, over his shoulders, and it was impossible to think when all of the blood in his head had drained down to his crotch. And the way she was rubbing against him, she had to know it.

He pressed his mouth to the side of her jaw. Her skin was hot and her pulse was racing. There was no doubt that she was as aroused as he was, that she wanted him as much as he wanted her. But was it real—or had he interrupted some kind of erotic dream?

He lifted his head reluctantly.

"Penny, we really should talk before—"

"I don't want to talk." She was already unbuttoning his shirt, those nimble fingers making quick work of the task.

Then her palms were splayed against his chest, and her touch against his bare skin was almost more than he could stand. Okay, so talking wasn't really what he wanted, either. "But—"

"Shut up, Jason." She captured his mouth again, her teeth sinking into his bottom lip.

Jason shut up and kissed her.

She managed to push his shirt over his shoulders and down his arms, then reached for the button at the front of his pants. He rolled off of the bed and shucked his clothes. Penny propped herself up on her elbows to watch him. Her face was flushed, her eyes dark, her lips swollen from his kisses.

"Your turn," he told her.

Not so very long ago, she would have balked at the request, too shy and self-conscious to comply. But in the time that they'd spent together, he'd helped her to explore and enjoy her own body, and she'd quickly learned how to wield her newly discovered feminine power.

She shifted so that she was kneeling in the center of the bed, then she bunched the bottom of the gown in her fists and slowly slid it upward, revealing just the tiniest glimpse of the pale, smooth skin of her thighs, then a tiny bit more.

He wanted her naked. Now. But he remained standing by the edge of the bed—his hands curled into fists to prevent himself from reaching for her and tearing the gown from her body—and let her tease him.

When the hem of the gown finally reached her hips, he caught a glimpse of cream-colored lace, then more pale skin. Her previously flat belly was now gently curved, and this evidence of their baby growing inside of her made her pregnancy suddenly and shockingly real to him. But as the fabric continued its upward journey, inch by torturous inch, he forgot about the baby and thought only of Penny. Finally, she whisked the gown over her head and tossed it to the floor, on top of the pile of clothes he'd discarded.

She held out her hand to him, and then he was back on the bed with her. Kissing her and touching her. And she was kissing and touching him. He knew how to take things slow, how to draw out a moment and pleasure a woman.

But Penny had her own ideas this time. Her tongue plunged into his mouth, her nails scraped down his back, her body arched against his, urging him on. And, well, what was a guy supposed to do, when he had a warm, willing woman writhing beneath him?

He rose up and plunged into her.

He didn't worry about a condom. What was the point, when she was already carrying his child? But without any kind of barrier between them, she seemed hotter, wetter, tighter than he remembered.

She cried out with shocked pleasure and began to move, pumping her hips in rhythm with his own.

It was rough and fast and just a little bit wild.

She draped her arms over his shoulders, her nails biting into his flesh. He scraped his teeth over her collarbone, nipped at her throat. She locked her legs around his waist, pulling him even deeper inside. His fingers dug into her hips as he drove her closer and closer to the peak.

And then her body convulsed around him, clamping tight like a velvet fist, and dragging him over the edge with her.

Penny lay motionless beneath Jason's warm and familiar weight. Her body was more than satisfied; her mind was spinning. She'd just had incredible, mind-numbing, body-melting sex, which should have been a cause for celebration rather than concern.

But when that mind-numbing, body-melting sex had been with a man whom she'd vowed to cut out of her life, things changed. A lot. When that man also happened to be the father of her baby, the situation got even more complicated.

She'd known exactly what she was doing when she'd kissed him. She'd wanted this to happen, she wanted a chance to say goodbye on her terms. But she'd failed to

fully consider the ramifications of her actions, to antici-
pate that making love with him again would make it
harder for her to break the emotional ties.

It seemed as if she'd made one mistake after another when it came to Jason Foley, but this was where
it would end.

When he rolled off of her but tried to snuggle her
close against his body, she held herself still. She'd been
surprised, pleasantly so, when she'd first realized that
the tough, implacable businessman was not just an incredibly considerate lover but a cuddler, and almost as
much as she'd loved making love with him, she'd loved
cuddling up with him after making love.

Of course, that was when she believed that they were
making love. The knowledge that he'd only been using
her had tainted all of her memories.

He pressed his lips to the back of her shoulder, and
though she couldn't prevent the goose bumps that rose
up on her skin, she didn't allow herself any other reaction.

"I missed you, Penny."

His voice was husky. The words sounded sincere. But
Penny was no longer the naive virgin who had been
easily duped by this man before. She certainly wasn't
going to be duped again.

She extricated herself from his embrace and re-
trieved her discarded clothes from the floor. Because
her knees were still trembling, she had to sit on the edge
of the bed to put her panties back on. When he stroked
a hand lazily down her back, his fingertips trailing
down the line of her spine, she felt tears prick the back
of her eyes.

She'd missed him, too. She'd missed the sound of his

voice, the warmth of his laughter and the way his eyes lit up when he saw her, as if her presence had truly brightened his day. She'd missed the sense of companionship, the pleasure she derived just from being with him, whether they were sharing a romantic dinner or watching a late-night movie on television or shopping for groceries. And she'd missed his touch, the casual brushes and seductive caresses, and especially the way he was touching her now.

Their lovemaking had been not just amazing but incredibly varied, and she'd been both awed and overwhelmed to experience the unexpected heights of passion. Whether their coming together had been leisurely and tender or fast and hard, he'd always made her feel wanted. And afterward, when he held her close, he'd made her feel cherished.

Irritated with herself for the self-indulgent trek down memory lane, she yanked her nightgown down over her head, thrust her arms into the sleeves and stood up.

"It was sex," she said, aiming for a dismissive tone to disguise the tightness in her throat. "Don't try to make it into anything bigger than that."

"Just sex?"

She had no trouble hearing the annoyance—and anger—in his question.

She lifted a shoulder, determined to play it casual, to not let him know how much the experience had shaken her. "Apparently, all the hormones that flood a women's system during pregnancy can really jump-start her libido. Obviously, that's what happened."

"So it had nothing to do with the history or attraction between you and me?" The words were bit out between clenched teeth as he dressed. "I was just convenient?"

"Don't go getting all indignant," she warned. "I'm sure, from time to time, you've done it with a woman just because she was there and she was willing."

His gaze narrowed dangerously. "We're not talking about me, though, are we? We're talking about you, and you were a twenty-six-year-old virgin until I took you to my bed a few months ago."

"Did I forget to thank you for that?" she asked. "Because it really was an incredible night."

"I'm not asking for a damn thank you."

"Well, I'm grateful anyway," she said. "And for everything that came after, I'm doubly grateful, because I really don't think I ever would have known what selfish bastards men could be without your experienced tutelage in that regard."

"You're really starting to piss me off," he warned her.

"So it's okay for you to use me for your own purposes, but it's not okay for me to call you on it?"

She saw the muscle in his jaw flex as he clamped it tight, and when he finally spoke, it was in what she referred to as his boardroom voice.

"I think we're getting a little off-topic," he said, his tone both cool and reasonable.

"It was a bad idea to try to talk about this tonight," she responded levelly. "I'm exhausted, which is apparently normal in the first trimester of any pregnancy, but which is unusual for me. I'm also cranky because my whole life is about to change and I haven't quite figured out exactly how I'm going to manage those changes. So if you don't mind, I'd really like to postpone any further conversation until we've both had a chance to think about everything."

"Of course," he agreed solicitously. "But for the record, you mean a lot more to me than you obviously realize."

She wanted to believe him, but she wasn't going to be fooled again. "For the record, I won't ever trust anything you say to me again."

Chapter Four

Jason wasn't in a good mood the next morning.

Of course, being awakened by an urgent call from his secretary after a mostly sleepless night had done nothing to establish a positive outlook for his day. And the cold shoulder he'd been getting from Penny since he crossed paths with her in the kitchen when he went to grab a cup of coffee did nothing to improve things.

How could she have been so hot for him last night and completely oblivious to his presence less than eight hours later?

"All the hormones that flood a women's system during pregnancy can really jump-start her libido. Obviously, that's what happened."

Though her words came back to haunt him, he didn't believe them any more now than he had when she'd thrown them at him the night before.

He did believe that she would spend the whole day pretending he wasn't there, if he let her. But he had no intention of fading into the background just because it was what Penny wanted. And he sure as hell had no intention of denying that it was his baby she was carrying.

Unfortunately, he spent most of the morning on the phone with either his secretary or the assistant VP of an associate office in Denver, but while he went through the motions, his mind was preoccupied with that little bombshell that Penny had dropped on him the previous evening. It occurred to him that he could more quickly and easily deal with the unexpected office crisis if he actually went back to the office, but he had no intention of leaving before he and Penny had come to some kind of agreement with respect to their child.

Of course, she'd actually have to talk to him in order for that to happen, but he remained optimistic. Or maybe it was more accurate to say he was determined.

So, when they were once again all gathered around the big tables set up in Travis's dining room, plates overflowing with slices of turkey and ham and mounds of mashed potatoes and stuffing dripping with gravy, Jason considered his plan.

A plan that got an unexpected boost when his father rose to his feet.

"Since we are all gathered around to celebrate Thanksgiving, I think it's a good time to reflect on the many reasons we are thankful. Throughout my life, I have been blessed with a wonderful family, good health and good fortune. But this year, I have even more reason to be thankful, and that reason is the beautiful bride sitting beside me."

"I don't see a bride." Livie was the first to respond to the announcement.

"I think your grandpa's telling us that he and Mrs. McCord got married," Zane explained to his daughter.

"It's Mrs. Foley now," Rex said proudly. "But you can call her Grandma."

"Or just 'Eleanor'," his wife said, apparently not wanting to push the child to accept her in the unaccustomed role too soon.

"Well, I guess congratulations are in order," Charlie said, though he sounded a little dubious as he lifted his glass.

Not to be outdone, the rest of the McCords and the Foleys followed suit.

"Congratulations."

"May you have a long, happy life together."

"To the bride and groom."

Though toasts rang out amid the clinking of crystal, Jason knew that not everyone was thrilled by the union. Or maybe it would just take a while for both families to accept that the ancient feud was truly at an end, as symbolized by Rex and Eleanor's marriage.

"While we're celebrating good news," Jason began, rising to his feet to address the group crowded around the table. "I have some of my own to share."

The conversations around him slowly died away, the clink of silverware ceased as all eyes focused on him. All eyes including Penny's green ones—which were wide and panicked when they locked on his.

She gave a slight shake of her head, a silent, desperate plea. Apparently she'd finally given up trying to pretend he didn't exist, an illusion that he'd already decided to put an end to in a big way.

"I'm going to be a father." He looked across the table at the expectant mother. "Penny is going to have my baby."

Penny wasn't surprised that Jason's proclamation was met with stunned silence.

Although her sister, her mother and, since last night, Gabby, were aware of her pregnancy, no one else had any idea about the extent of her relationship with Jason.

"Yay, another baby," Livie said, clapping her hands.

She was shushed by her father, who obviously didn't share the child's enthusiasm for the proclamation.

Nor, it seemed, did anyone else around the table.

"I would expect that kind of news to be followed by the announcement of your impending wedding date." Though Rex's comment was directed to his son, Penny was the one who wanted to crawl under the table and hide.

This was exactly why she hadn't wanted to make a public announcement about her pregnancy—because she wasn't prepared to answer all of the questions she knew her well-meaning but interfering family would inevitably have. And obviously Jason's family was no different.

"Penny and I have a lot of plans to make," Jason said, deflecting rather than answering the question implied by his father's statement.

Rex looked as if he was about to say something more, but to Penny's surprise, her mother touched his sleeve and signaled him with a subtle shake of her head.

There were other murmurs and questions, but Penny let Jason respond to them. And then Paige, sensing her sister's quiet desperation, took advantage of a lull and diverted the conversation by asking Blake about his plans for marketing the McCordite.

While there was no further mention of her pregnancy during the meal, she was conscious of the attention focused on her…and the speculation. When dinner was finally over and Penny had started to clear away the dishes again, Blake came into the kitchen and took her by the arm.

"Walk with me," he said.

It wasn't a question but a directive, and though Penny wanted to balk at being ordered around like a recalcitrant child, she welcomed the opportunity to escape the suddenly cloying atmosphere of Travis's home.

"You can save the lecture, Blake," she said, when they were outside. "It's a little too late to warn me about the dangers of unprotected sex."

"If I was going to lecture, it would be about the dangers of Jason Foley," he told her. "But under the circumstances, I won't bother."

"Thanks," she said dryly.

They walked in silence for a few minutes and Penny found the crisp air both refreshing and relaxing. For the first time, she really looked around, and she was pleased with what she saw. Travis obviously took pride in the land and Penny guessed her sister had probably fallen in love with the ranch, as well as the rancher.

"Have you thought about how you're going to handle things?"

Blake's question drew her attention away from the distant horizon and back to more immediate problems.

"I haven't been able to think about anything else," she admitted. "Not that I've come up with any answers."

"Are you going to marry Jason?"

"No," she answered that question quickly, adamantly.

"Have you told him that?"

"What makes you think he wants to marry me? Other than his father wanting him to do so."

"Don't underestimate family pressure," Blake warned her. "But aside from that, he's a successful businessman, a pillar in the community. He'll want to do the right thing, and in his mind, that is marrying the mother of his child."

Something in his tone—or maybe it was her understanding of their family history—made her ask, "You don't think it's the right thing, do you?"

"No, I don't," he told her. "I don't think you'll do yourself or your child any favors by marrying a man you don't love just to give him a father."

She knew, when Blake said "him," he wasn't necessarily referring to her child, but to the child *he* had been, and she knew he'd been badly hurt by their mother's coolness toward him.

It was only in recent years that he realized Eleanor had always resented him, albeit subconsciously, for being the reason she had to marry Devon McCord. And though she'd remained married and had gone on to have three more children with him, the shadows of that initial resentment had never quite faded away.

"I didn't plan on getting pregnant at this point in my life," Penny admitted to Blake. "But I love this baby already, and I promise you that I will never blame him— or her—for the circumstances of conception."

Her brother nodded. "You'll be a good mom, Penny."

Mom. The word created flutters of both excitement and apprehension in her belly. "I hope so."

"And if you ever need anything, just let me know."

She managed a smile. "Like a babysitter?"

"I'm not sure you'd want me to babysit," he warned her. Then, more seriously, "But I mean it, Pen. I don't want you to feel as if you need to count on Jason Foley for anything. Me and Tate and Paige, we're your family. You can depend on us."

"I know," she said, and hugged him tight.

And while she appreciated that her brother had the best of intentions, she knew she couldn't cut Jason Foley out of the equation as easily as Blake had implied.

While Penny was walking with Blake, Jason went outside for some air and was cornered by Gabby on the front porch.

"You do know you didn't earn any points by publicly announcing Penny's pregnancy, don't you?"

He shrugged. "I was making a point."

"That you're too stupid to think about birth control?" She smiled sweetly. "I'm sorry, did I say that out loud?"

"I appreciate that you feel protective of your cousin, but I'm not going to discuss my relationship with Penny with you."

"You're the one who put it on the table—literally. And did you even *think* about the fact that Tanya Kimbrough is a reporter before you decided to make your big announcement?"

He scowled, because he hadn't. "A reporter who happens to be engaged to Penny's brother."

"Do you think that connection is going to make her withhold that kind of news?"

"Okay, I didn't think," he admitted. "I just wanted

Penny to know that I'm accepting responsibility for my child."

"How far are you willing to go to accept that responsibility?"

"Did you hear me say I wasn't going to discuss this with you?"

She waved a hand dismissively, like the blue-blood heiress she was. "I just want to make sure that you've considered all of the angles."

"I'm working on it."

"Including the negative publicity that this news could generate for both the Foley and McCord families?"

"Penny's pregnancy is hardly newsworthy."

"You don't think so?" she challenged.

"She's neither royalty nor a celebrity," he said, but he couldn't deny that Gabby had a lot of experience with the media, and if she was concerned, maybe he should be, too.

"Your brother and Penny's sister found the Santa Magdalena Diamond—that discovery alone is enough to have the press salivating like a pack of mangy dogs over a juicy bone. Not to mention that their appetites have already been whetted by the teaser pieces Tanya did about the Foleys and the McCords and the ancient feud. Now you can add in Travis and Paige's engagement and Rex and Eleanor's marriage, and the paparazzi will be foaming at their mouths to find yet another meaty morsel of gossip to devour."

"I suppose you have some advice on how we should handle it?"

She nodded. "Marry her. Give her—and your baby—legitimacy. Don't let them turn Penny into a dirty little secret and your child into a mistake."

"I mentioned marriage," he admitted. "Penny didn't seem interested."

"You're Chief Operating Officer of Foley Industries. I'm sure you didn't rise to that position without knowing how to overcome opposition, how to make things happen that others thought never would."

She was right. In fact, it was one of the reasons he'd been elected by his siblings to learn what he could about the McCords' search for the Santa Magdalena Diamond. Even if that mission hadn't been a rousing success, at least insofar as finding the diamond was concerned.

But he had found Penny, and he'd lost her without understanding why. Of course, everything was clear to him now, and though he understood her reasons for withdrawing from him, he still wasn't ready to give up on her, on what they'd shared together. And now that he knew she was carrying his child, he was even less willing to let her go.

Gabby was right—he knew how to make things happen.

And he was going to make Penny McCord his wife.

Penny was zipping up her duffel bag when the knock sounded on the door.

"Come in," she said, because she assumed it was her sister. Because she assumed that Jason wouldn't have the nerve to come looking for her after what he'd done.

Then he stepped through the door, and she realized she'd assumed incorrectly.

He looked at the bag, then at her. "You're leaving?"

"Your powers of deductive reasoning are amazing."

"Because of me?"

"Believe it or not, Jason, the world doesn't revolve around you."

She reached for her bag, but he grabbed the handle first.

"I'd like you to stay," he said. "Just through the weekend, so that we can figure some things out."

"Tomorrow is the busiest shopping day of the year, and I need to be at the store."

"You work on the design end, and you can sketch anywhere. At least, that's what you used to say when you spent weekends at my penthouse in Houston," he reminded her.

She used to say a lot of things—and so did he. But she refused to go down that road with him. "There are times when I need to be available for customer consultations. This is one of those times."

He didn't look happy with her response, but he was in no position to refute her argument. "I could come to the city for the weekend," he offered instead.

"I appreciate that you're making an effort, but the fact is, I'm going to be busy all weekend, and it would be a waste of your time to come to Dallas if your only purpose is to badger me."

He ran a hand through his hair, a rare gesture of impatience. "I have to go out of town on Monday."

"You don't have to account for your whereabouts to me," she told him.

He ignored the edge in her voice. "I'll be gone most of next week, but when I get back, we'll make plans to talk."

"Talk? As in discuss? Because as far as I can tell, you don't discuss anything. You make decisions and act upon them, regardless of the impact on anyone else."

"You're annoyed that I announced your pregnancy to

our families," Jason guessed. And maybe he had over-played his hand there, but he wouldn't make the same mistake again.

"It wasn't your announcement to make."

"It's my baby, too."

"As if I could forget," she muttered.

"How many times do I have to say I'm sorry?"

"You can say it as many times as you want, but those two little words can't undo what you did."

"You're right," he agreed. "So why don't we put the past behind us and move forward?"

"I am moving forward," she told him. "And I'm doing it without you."

"Come on, Penny. Have you never made a mistake? Done something you regretted?"

She met his gaze evenly. "Yes, I have."

He forced himself to remember that he knew how to overcome opposition, even if he wasn't accustomed to that opposition being presented in such a maddeningly attractive package.

"I know you're angry with me," he said reasonably. "And you have every right to be. But I'm not going to let you cut me out of our baby's life."

"You don't want this baby, Jason. Why are you pre-tending otherwise?"

"How do you know what I want?" he challenged.

"Okay, maybe I should have said that you didn't plan this baby."

"Neither of us did."

"And if I wasn't pregnant, you wouldn't be here right now."

"But you are pregnant," he pointed out.

"Maybe you should put it on a billboard," she said, yanking the handle of her bag from his hand and slinging it over her shoulder. "Because it's possible there are still some people in the great state of Texas who haven't actually heard you shout out the news yet."

He realized that both of their voices had risen and he deliberately lowered his when he responded.

"Obviously, we both need some time to think about things. We'll continue this discussion when I get back next week. But while I'm gone," he continued, in what he thought was a perfectly calm and reasonable tone, "I want you to think about a wedding date."

"You don't want to marry me, you want the baby. And Jason Foley doesn't give up on anything he wants."

"You'd be wise to remember that," he told her.

"How could I forget, when that's what got me into this situation?"

"Maybe there's something else you've forgotten," he said, and crushed his mouth to hers in a hard, punishing kiss.

Penny kept her lips tightly clamped together. No way was she going to respond to such Neanderthal tactics.

But then his lips softened, moving more persuasively than persistently now, and it was just like the first time he kissed her…

Chapter Five

Penny hadn't really wanted to attend Missy Harcourt's wedding. Though they'd attended the same private schools and moved in the same social circles throughout the years, she and the bride had never been particularly close. But it was important, her mother said, for there to be a representative of the McCord family at the wedding, since the Harcourts were old friends of the family. Since Penny was the only one who didn't already have plans for the day in question, she was nominated.

When she complained about attending the event alone, Tate had mentioned that he had a colleague who was interested in going out with her. It turned out that Doctor Edmond Lang had actually been hoping to score a date with Paige, but, as Penny's outgoing twin never had any trouble lining up her own escorts, had been persuaded to settle for Penny. Not that either Tate or Edmond admitted as much, but her date calling her Paige—not once but three times—was a pretty big clue.

In any event, when Dr. Lang was paged by the hospital just as dessert was being cleared away, Penny wasn't overly disappointed. And she figured losing her date was a valid excuse for her to cut out early, too. In fact, she was on her way to the hotel concierge desk to request a taxi when she saw him across the hotel lobby.

Jason Foley. Of the infamous Foleys, sworn enemies of the McCord family since the Civil War. While the Foleys and the McCords were unlikely to issue challenges of pistols at dawn to one another in the current day, they were just as unlikely to cross a room to say hello to a member of the other family. But that knowledge had never prevented Penny from admiring any of the very handsome Foley brothers from afar. And Jason Foley—the second of Rex Foley's three sons—was the one she'd admired the most. All six-foot-two, Colin-Farrell-look-alike yumminess of him.

Her heart gave a little bump against her ribs.

It wasn't fair that a mortal enemy should look so darn good, or that she should be so attracted to a man who would never look twice in her direction.

She'd seen him at various society events over the years, but never had he given her more than a passing glance. This time, however, his eyes locked on hers—and held.

Penny's heart gave another, harder bump.

Then he crossed the room, actually going out of his way to approach her. Had there been anyone else in the vicinity, she would never have made such an assumption, but all of the other guests were still inside the main ballroom.

"You're not trying to duck out already, are you, Penny?"

The deep baritone voice skimmed over her skin like a caress, raising goose bumps on her flesh. But it was his use of her name that nearly made her knees buckle. Not even her own date had remembered she wasn't her sister—or maybe he hadn't wanted to remember. But Jason had somehow known who she was and had sought her out anyway...

Her pulse was racing now, but she lifted one shoulder, deliberately casual, determined not to let him see how much he'd flustered her. *"My date had an emergency and—"*

"I didn't come with a date," he interrupted smoothly. *"So I would be incredibly grateful if you'd take a turn with me on the dance floor."*

He wanted to dance...with her?

"I appreciate the invitation, Mr. Foley, but—"

"Jason," he said, interrupting her again. *"And the way to show your appreciation would be to accept the invitation."*

Penny took his proffered hand and hoped he didn't notice that her fingers trembled.

It was, after all, only a dance.

But even when the dance was over, he didn't leave her side. It was only when the bride and groom had departed that she realized they'd been talking for a long time, and while she was reluctant for the evening to end, she knew that she should be getting home.

Jason seemed equally reluctant to say good-night, and when she politely declined his offer to go somewhere for coffee, he insisted on at least giving her a ride *home. That offer she accepted, simply because it was more expedient than waiting for a taxi.*

And then he insisted on seeing her to the door. Jason Foley walked her right up to the front door of her parents' house and lightning didn't strike.

And then he kissed her. And she thought maybe she'd been wrong about the lightning, because the moment his lips touched hers, something jolted through her system and singed her right down to her toes.

And with that first kiss, he'd completely swept her off her feet.

Of course, Penny still hadn't believed anything more would ever come of it. Or maybe it was more accurate to say she hadn't dared let herself hope anything would come of it. Because although his kiss had awakened every hormone in her body, it was still just a kiss. Sure, no one had ever kissed her with such tenderness and passion before, but she was certain Jason Foley had kissed a thousand women in just the same way.

Okay, maybe not a *thousand,* but the man did have something of a reputation. And he'd dated a *lot* of women. Glamorous and sophisticated women. And while Penny knew she wasn't the ugly stepsister—how could she be when she looked exactly like her twin?— her innate shyness frequently relegated her to the shadows behind her fabulous and outgoing sister.

When she didn't hear from Jason the next day, she wasn't surprised. Obviously, he'd been bored at the wedding and was simply toying with her.

But the day after that he *did* call, and he invited her to grab a cup of coffee. She had been as excited as she was surprised by the invitation, and happily agreed. Somehow, coffee had led to dinner. And during that first dinner, all of her preconceived notions about him—and about herself—went flying out the window.

And so began their relationship.

She'd had boyfriends before—she wasn't a complete neophyte when it came to dating. But she'd never had a relationship that made her feel so good about who she was, and so optimistic about the future. She had never felt anything like she felt when she was with Jason.

With every date, every touch and every kiss, she fell a little bit deeper and harder for the handsome executive. It wasn't just flattering to have a man like Jason Foley interested in her, it was mind-boggling. But Penny had been too thrilled that he was, to question why.

For the first time in her life, she hadn't been the "youngest daughter" or someone's "sister" or "Paige's twin"—she'd been her own person. She'd been the woman Jason Foley chose to be with.

The only factor that took some of the shine off her happy glow was that she couldn't tell anyone they were dating. She didn't dare.

Growing up in Devon McCord's home meant that "Foley" was a taboo F-word, so she'd kept their relationship a secret.

Until one night at dinner, frustrated by the patronizing attitudes of her family, she blurted out the truth. Even then, she wasn't sure anyone believed her relationship with Jason was serious, and—in retrospect—the doubts had been well founded.

But Penny had romanticized the obstacles she and Jason faced, believing they were star-crossed lovers, like Romeo and Juliet. But she'd trusted that their attraction was stronger than the influence of their respective families, stronger than a silly old feud.

Then she learned that their entire relationship had been fuelled by that feud, by Jason's determination to ensure that the Foleys finally bested the McCords. She'd been falling in love and he'd been digging for information.

And still, it seemed as if she'd learned nothing from the experience. Because all it took was a look, a touch, a kiss, and she was like putty in his hands, willing to forget everything he'd done and give him another chance.

But another chance for what? To break her heart? Or to be a father to their baby? Because if he wanted to be part of their baby's life, then he would inevitably be part of her life, too. And how the heck was she supposed to deal with that?

She should hate him. She *wanted* to hate him.

But in her heart, she couldn't forget how wonderful he'd been.

Maybe it had all been an act, but her heart wasn't entirely convinced. Deep inside, she clung to the belief that if all he'd wanted from her was information, he could have found out what she knew—which was actually nothing—over the occasional cup of coffee. But the first cup of coffee had led to an invitation to dinner, and dinner had led to more kissing, and maybe she was guilty of having her head in the clouds, but she was pretty sure she would have remembered if he'd been asking about diamonds and querying her on the McCord finances while they were naked together.

And that was what she kept coming back to, the hope

that refused to die, the belief that, regardless of Jason's motives, he had grown to care about her.

Or maybe she *was* as pathetically naive as everyone believed her to be.

Although Jason had cursed—loudly and creatively— while he'd been making plans to go to Denver to untangle a mess that had been left behind by the now-departed VP, he realized that a few days away would give him the time and distance he needed to really think about Penny's pregnancy and make plans for their future.

If he wasn't quite ready to be a father, he knew he had no one but himself to blame, and that he obviously should have given the matter some thought before he got naked with Penny. Not that he'd simply disregarded the use of birth control. No way—he was smarter than that.

Unfortunately, he was *not* smart enough to realize that when a woman with decidedly less experience assured him that she was "safe," they might be thinking different things. And he was *not* smart enough to have known that when she hesitated before saying she didn't sleep around, what she really meant was that she'd never been with a man before.

And despite this miscommunication, he was the villain because he'd seduced sweet, innocent Penny McCord.

Okay, so she was sweet—probably the sweetest woman he'd ever known.

And she had been innocent.

She'd also been willing and eager, sexy and seductive, and incredibly and passionately responsive…

After weeks of long late-night telephone conversations and occasional stolen moments when Jason was in Dallas, he'd finally convinced Penny to come to Houston for a weekend. He told her about a new dance club that had opened up and that he was anxious to check out, and how he really hoped she would go with him. When she'd hesitated, he hastened to assure her that he had a guest room in his penthouse, and she'd finally agreed.

It was nearly eight o'clock when the doorman called to tell him that he had a guest. While Penny was riding the elevator to the twenty-second floor, Jason uncorked the chardonnay he'd chilled and poured two glasses. They would have a drink, nibble on the fruit and cheese he'd set out, share some conversation, then head out around ten.

His plan flew out the door when he opened it and saw her standing there.

He'd always known she was attractive. Though she had a tendency to downplay her natural prettiness, there was no disguising the luster of her long red-gold hair or the sparkle in her deep green eyes. But in the little black dress that was more little than dress, with her hair spilling down her back in wildly spiraling curls, she wasn't downplaying anything tonight. In fact, her mile-long legs were shown to full advantage in the short skirt and sexy heels that brought her five-foot-eight-inch frame to a height that nearly matched his own, putting that slick, glossy mouth in direct line with his.

"I opened a bottle of wine," he said, finally recovering enough to speak. "But you look as if you're ready to go."

"Wine would be nice." She took the glass from his hand, lifted it to her lips. She sipped, then traced her tongue over her lower lip. "Yes, very nice."

He swallowed hard as two thoughts battled for su-

premacy inside his addled brain: "what happened to sweet Penny McCord?" and "how soon could he get her naked?"

"Are you hungry?" he asked. "Because we could go out for a bite before we head to the club."

He hadn't forgotten about the fruit and cheese, he just figured it would be smarter to go out to eat, to leave the penthouse. Now. Or they might not leave at all.

He didn't know if she read his mind or if she simply wanted the same thing he did, because she said, "Actually, I was thinking that maybe we could stay in."

"Oh. Well." He sounded like an idiot, but he found it difficult to form words with his tongue tied in knots. "I thought you wanted to go to the club."

"I thought you could give me a tour of your place...including the guest room I have no intention of sleeping in."

Well, he didn't need to be hit over the head. Not more than once, anyway.

He took the forgotten glass of wine from her hand and set it aside, then he reached for her.

They came together, hearts pounding, mouths fusing, bodies straining.

It was crazy. Even while it was happening, he knew it was crazy. He hadn't been so desperately aroused since...he didn't even know since when. Probably since he was in tenth grade and Nadia Sinclair let him unfasten her bra, beginning a lifelong fascination with female breasts.

As his mouth fastened over Penny's tight nipple through the fabric of her dress, he couldn't help but think that Nadia had nothing on Penny McCord. And then he wasn't thinking about anything but Penny.

Somehow, they made it down the hall to his bedroom. Her dress was on the floor, along with a couple of pieces of skimpy satin and lace that probably deserved more attention than he'd paid to them in the few seconds it took him to strip them away. But he paid a great deal of attention to the long, lean, completely naked and very sexy body that was stretched out across his king-size mattress.

They'd been moving toward this moment for weeks. But even so, he hadn't expected to be so frantic and needy. And if her moans and sighs were any indication, she was as desperate for their joining as he was. He shed the last of his clothes and joined her on the bed. Her arms came around him, drawing him close, closer.

He was teetering on the edge of no return when he pulled back. His breathing was harsh and ragged, his body screaming for release inside of her.

Her eyes flickered, opened, revealing that deep green, dark with desire, clouded with confusion.

"What's wrong?"

What was wrong was that he wanted to plunge inside her hot, wet body more than he wanted to take his next breath, but caution—or maybe it was a finely honed self-protection instinct—had managed to pierce the sexual haze that clouded his brain.

"I wasn't prepared for this," he admitted, inwardly cursing himself for the oversight. But he'd never expected things to go so far so fast. Yeah, he had plans for the weekend, and he'd hoped those plans would lead to this moment. But not before he had a chance

to stop at the pharmacy, which he was going to do on the way home from the club. Except that they'd never gone out to the club, and he'd never expected to want her so much.

"Please tell me you have some protection?" It was a plea, heartfelt and desperate.

She blinked, uncomprehending.

"Condoms," he clarified.

She shook her head, then ventured, hesitantly. "I don't...sleep around, Jason. I'm...safe."

Which he'd assumed to mean that she was on the pill or using the patch or some other form of birth control. And since he hadn't had unprotected sex in more than a decade because he cared more about his long-term health than short-term gratification, he trusted that he wasn't putting her at risk....

Obviously, he'd been wrong. And while the details had yet to be determined, the one thing Jason knew for certain was that the baby Penny carried meant they were now bound together in ways he never intended.

He'd always expected that he would marry and become a father someday, and though he hadn't expected it to happen so soon, he wasn't bothered by the acceleration of his plans. After all, it wasn't as if he'd been waiting to fall in love. No, he'd been there, done that, and had no intention of repeating that painful experience again. But he did care about Penny, and he was confident they could have a good life together.

Of course, the biggest challenge would be in convincing Penny to marry him. He'd seen the look on her face when his father mentioned a wedding date, and he knew she wouldn't want to get married simply because she was pregnant.

But a baby needed two parents—he didn't think that belief was old-fashioned so much as it was practical. And he wanted to be involved in every aspect of his child's life, which meant being there when his child went to bed at night and when he or she woke up in the morning. He was a little less enthused about the prospect of midnight feedings and dirty diapers, but he was willing to share those responsibilities, too.

In fact, he was willing to do almost anything to make Penny his bride.

Anything but open up his heart to a woman who already meant more to him than he'd ever intended.

Chapter Six

Penny picked up the raw piece of McCordite and turned it over in her hand, watching the subtle shift of shimmery colors. It was a truly unique gem, and she was thrilled to have the chance to play with it, to experiment with designs and metals to show it to full advantage.

Images swirled through her mind like pictures on a carousel. Her pieces would be the latest rage, worn by the wealthiest women with the most discriminating tastes: the wives of old fortunes and new entrepreneurs, the mistresses of European royalty, the names that topped Hollywood's A-list.

She never lacked for inspiration in her designs, and she could already picture elegant pendants and jewel-studded chokers, dangling earrings and thick, chunky bracelets. There was so much she could and would do with the stone, but her first task—and undoubtedly the most difficult one—was her sister's engagement ring.

It was part of her usual process to meet with a customer prior to the design of a custom piece. She believed it was important for a gift of jewelry to reflect something of the person who would wear it, of the relationship between the gift giver and the recipient.

She shouldn't have to interview her sister or have her sister's fiancé complete a questionnaire, but she couldn't deny that she was…well, *blocked* seemed the most appropriate word for what she was feeling. She was trying—really she was—but every time she closed her eyes and envisioned Travis sliding the ring on Paige's finger, her own eyes filled with tears, blurring the image, so that the inspiration she sought remained elusive.

It was shamefully obvious to Penny that she was envious of her sister. She was genuinely happy for Paige, thrilled that her dreams were coming true. And though she didn't know Travis well, it was readily apparent that he adored Paige. Yes, Penny was happy for them—even if, right now, she was feeling absolutely miserable, because she so desperately wanted what they had found.

She set the rock back on her desk and wiped at the tears that had overflowed and slid down her cheeks. She wasn't a crier, not usually, but lately it seemed as if the littlest thing could set off the waterworks. She knew it was the pregnancy that was responsible for her hormones being so completely out of whack, but that knowledge didn't assuage the ache in her heart.

The ring of the phone jolted her back to the present,

and she grabbed for the receiver, grateful for the reprieve from the dangerously seductive memories—until she heard Jason's voice on the other end.

"I just wanted to give you the number of my hotel in Denver," he told her. "In case you needed to get in touch with me while I'm away."

She waved a hand in front of her face, trying to cool her suddenly heated skin. Yeah, those pregnancy hormones were definitely running rampant, when just the sound of his voice made everything inside her quiver.

"I'm not going to need to get in touch with you," she assured him, her tone carefully neutral. "And if I did, I have your cell number."

"Oh. Right."

"So why did you really call, Jason?"

"Would you believe I just wanted to hear the sound of your voice?"

"No."

His voice dropped, the low, intimate tone sending shivers down her spine. "I have missed you, Penny."

She steeled herself against the weakness that washed through her. She didn't know what game he was playing now, but she wasn't playing it with him. Not this time. "You saw me yesterday."

"I wish you were here with me now," he said. "Just the two of us."

She closed her eyes and tried to ignore the seductive words, reminding herself that it had never really been just the two of them—that Jason's hidden agenda had always been with them. "I have to go."

"Wait, Penny. Please—"

She couldn't wait, because she didn't trust herself not to respond to the plea in his voice.

Instead, she hung up on him.

Jason stared at the buzzing receiver in his hand.

She'd actually hung up on him.

His first response was disbelief, then annoyance, which was ultimately followed by relief. Because he knew that Penny wouldn't have disconnected so abruptly unless she was feeling confused and uncertain, unless she was worried that he might talk her into something she didn't want to be talked into. Something like…*marriage?*

Not that she was a pushover by any stretch of the imagination, and not that he'd ever had to talk her into anything. In fact, looking back on their brief relationship, he was hard-pressed to determine who'd been the pursuer and who'd been pursued. Yes, he'd been the one to approach her at the Harcourt-Ellsworth wedding, and he'd been the one to initiate the follow-up contact a couple of days later. But ultimately, she was the one who had seduced him.

Not that he'd resisted her seduction. Why would he, when he'd wanted her as much as she'd obviously wanted him? But the forthrightness and the passion she'd demonstrated that first night in Houston had created a sensual fog around his brain that kept him in the dark about a couple of key points—most notably that she was a virgin and that when she'd assured him she was "safe," she hadn't been referring to birth control.

That was the night their baby was conceived. He was certain of it, because he'd made a trip to the pharmacy the next morning. And though he'd resented the barrier he'd purposely put between them every time they made love thereafter, he'd never balked at doing so, because he didn't want to put her at risk.

Obviously, his precautions had been too little too late. And now…

He blew out a breath as he pulled out a suitcase and began to pack for his trip.

Now he couldn't blame her for being angry and wary.

He was the one who should have known better. He should have taken more care. And he should have let her know how much he cared, before everything blew up in his face.

Penny ignored the ringing phone. She didn't want to talk to Jason or about Jason or her baby, and she just wished everyone would leave her alone until she figured out what she was going to do.

If she had a choice, she would cut all ties with Jason Foley. But while she recognized that might give her a certain amount of satisfaction in the short term, it was hardly a viable solution for the long term. Because, as hurt and angry as she was over his treatment of her, there was a much more important consideration: her baby.

Jason's baby.

Her hand automatically went to her tummy, to the slight swelling that was already evident there, proof of the tiny life growing inside of her.

All of the pregnancy info she'd read on the Internet claimed that first pregnancies usually didn't start show-ing until the second trimester. Of course, most women lost a few pounds in the early months as a result of morning sickness, but Penny hadn't experienced any nausea, except when she was hungry.

So it seemed that she'd been eating almost constantly, and instead of the three to five pounds she should have put on by this stage of her pregnancy, she'd put on three *plus* five pounds. It was enough that she might have wondered if she was farther along in her pregnancy than the fourteen weeks she'd assumed, except that she'd been a virgin until fourteen weeks ago.

Because Penny was healthy and in good physical condition, the doctor had been surprised but not overly concerned, though she did warn the expectant mother to be careful as to how she satisfied her hunger. Apparently, chocolate chip cookie dough ice cream wasn't a pregnancy-approved breakfast food.

And now, here she was, eight pounds heavier, twenty-six years old, unmarried and pregnant.

Well, she could change the "unmarried" part if she wanted to. But Penny didn't want to marry a man who only wanted to marry her because he felt responsible. Maybe she'd been naive and idealistic to dream of falling in love and being loved in return, but she wasn't ready to give up on those dreams yet.

She felt the tears well up again and tried to blink them away. She'd never cried so much as she'd cried since the phone call from Paige that had decimated all of her hopes for a future with Jason. Because the future he was offering her now wasn't the one she wanted.

This time, when the phone started to ring, she glanced at the call display, frowning at the unfamiliar number. Even the area code wasn't one that she recognized. Out of state, she assumed, and the pieces clicked into place. Jason was in Denver. He called three times already from his cell phone—a number that she recogized—and she'd opted not to answer any of those calls. She just wasn't ready to talk to him, and she wasn't going to let him badger her into doing what he wanted when she still didn't have a clue what she wanted.

The phone finally stopped ringing when the answering machine picked up, and Penny held her breath, waiting. There was a pause, then a click, as the caller hung up without leaving a message.

She left her room and made her way to the kitchen.

Though she still lived at home and still slept in the same room she'd occupied while growing up, she'd never felt the urge to move out on her own, the need to experience greater freedom and independence. Maybe because her mother had always seemed to respect her space and never imposed unreasonable rules or curfews. Or maybe because the house was big enough that ten people could coexist peacefully without tripping over one another.

It occurred to her that she might have to rethink her living arrangements now that she was going to have a baby of her own. But right now she wasn't going to worry about anything, except what to have for dinner.

The phone in the kitchen was ringing when she made her way there, the same number showing on the display. Either Jason was trying to reach his father now or hoping to catch her on the main line. She waited for the ringing to stop, then took the receiver off the hook so she could have her dinner in peace.

She took a moment to study the contents of the refrigerator. As always, it was well stocked, but nothing really appealed to her. She opened the freezer, hoping for better prospects there, and found a tub of her favorite chocolate chip cookie dough ice cream.

She'd had the strangest cravings since she'd gotten pregnant—most notably, wanting ice cream at eight o'clock in the morning, every morning, salt and vinegar chips during a morning coffee break, oatmeal raisin cookies in the afternoon. Spinach salad was another new favorite, and while that was at least healthy, she didn't seem to be eating enough of it to counteract the effects of all the junk food. In fact, her pants were already feeling a little snug around the waist.

After only a few spoonfuls of the ice cream, she forced herself to put the tub back in the freezer and take out a box of fettuccine Alfredo with chicken and broccoli. Though JoBeth, the McCords longtime housekeeper, frowned on prepackaged meals of any kind, she did keep a stock of them in the freezer for Paige and Penny, for the nights she was off, of which tonight was one. It wasn't that the sisters couldn't cook, it was just that they rarely bothered to do so.

Penny nuked the pasta in its box, then dumped it into a bowl and sat down at the table. She was just finishing up her dinner when she heard footsteps in the hall. Since Eleanor had gone on a business trip with her new husband, and Paige had been staying with Travis at the ranch, Penny figured she had the house to herself.

She was surprised—but also grateful—when Paige came through the door. She could always count on her twin to distract her from her worries; and right now, she desperately needed a distraction from thoughts of Jason.

"I didn't really believe you were unconscious on the kitchen floor or trapped under a heavy piece of furniture," Paige said to her.

"Sorry to disappoint you," Penny said.

"Of course, I wouldn't have had to come all the way over here to prove it if you'd answered the phone."

"Did you call?"

"I tried, but the line was busy—" Paige arched a brow as she replaced the receiver on the wall "—and your cell went right to voice mail."

"I didn't want to talk to anyone," Penny said, feeling more than a little guilty at the thought that her sister had left her fiancé to check on her. "Did you come from the ranch?"

"I should let you think that I did," Paige said. "But I was coming into town anyway for an early meeting tomorrow."

"So why are you giving me such a hard time?"

"Because Jason has been trying to get in touch with you all day," her sister told her. "He was worried."

"Worried that I won't fall into line with what he wants," Penny muttered.

"You're pregnant," Paige said, as if Penny needed to be reminded of the fact. "You weren't answering your phone. Mom and Rex are out of town and JoBeth's not here. Is it so unbelievable that the father of your child might be concerned about you?"

"Is it so unbelievable that I might have been busy? Maybe I had errands to run—or went to see a movie."

"For five hours?"

Penny felt another twinge of guilt as she realized the

first call she'd ignored had come more than five hours earlier, but her willingness to talk to Jason hadn't changed in the time that had passed since then. "Maybe I had errands and then went to a movie."

Paige's cell rang and she flipped it open. "Yeah, I found her," she spoke into the phone. "Relatively unscathed. So far."

Penny deliberately tuned her out and dumped her empty pasta bowl in the sink. "If you only came over here to nag me, you can go now," she said, when Paige had ended her call.

Her sister sighed. "I know you're dealing with a lot of stuff right now—"

"Not really a lot," Penny denied. "Just one really big thing."

"I can't imagine what you're going through," her sister admitted. "But if there's anything I can do, or even if you just want to talk, you know I'm here for you."

"I do know, but there isn't anything. Unless you want to run interference and keep Jason out of my life while I figure things out?"

"Honey, I'm not sure even a bulldozer could keep Jason out of your life—or that it's a good idea."

"You never liked the idea of me dating him in the first place."

"That was before you got pregnant."

"You like him better now that you know he knocked me up?"

Paige rolled her eyes. "I'm just acknowledging that he is the father of your baby. And since he doesn't seem to be running from that responsibility, maybe you should give him a chance."

"A chance to do what? Stomp all over my heart again?"

"A chance to make things right."

"As if."

"You have every right to be angry and upset," Paige said. "But you're going to have to get past what he did for the sake of your child."

"I know," Penny agreed. "But it's not just that he used me or lied about his reasons for being with me."

"There's more?"

Penny nodded and went back to the freezer for the ice cream. She'd had the pasta, and there were even vegetables in it, and now the baby wanted ice cream. But she did get two spoons and gave one to her sister.

"I don't have a lot of experience with such situations, obviously, but when I told Jason that I was pregnant, I expected that he would try to deny it, or run from the room in a panic."

"Those would be typical male responses to news of an unplanned pregnancy," her sister agreed, dipping her own spoon into the tub.

"But not Jason's response," she told Paige. "As soon as I told him I was going to have his baby, he was immediately and completely focused on that. Okay, there was a moment—a flash of panic, or maybe it was horror in his eyes—but then it was gone and he was wanting to discuss options and make plans. I mean, I've had almost five weeks to accept it and my head is still reeling, but after five *minutes,* he's ready to calmly and rationally discuss our options."

"You're thinking he's a control freak like Dad," Paige guessed.

Penny nodded again.

"I can see why you'd be wary," her sister said. "We saw firsthand how Dad tried to control everyone. Not just Mom, but all of us. He was as ruthless in his personal relationships as he was in his business dealings, willing to do anything and everything to get what he wanted."

"Jason slept with me to get information about our family."

"I'm not going to deny that's true—how can I, when I was the one who found out what he was doing? But I am going to add a proviso to that."

"A proviso?" Penny managed to smile.

"Honey, whatever his reasons for taking you to his bed, he couldn't have faked what happened in that bed. And the fact that a man who is usually so cool and controlled overlooked something as basic as birth control—even on one occasion—tells me that he got a little carried away. And I assure you, that had nothing to do with the Santa Magdalena Diamond."

"The sex was good," Penny admitted, deciding it wasn't the time to enlighten her sister that she might have misled him on the subject of birth control, albeit inadvertently. Then she sighed. "Really good."

Paige grinned. "Then I'd have to say that some things do run in the family."

"Is that why you're marrying Travis?"

"I'm marrying Travis because he's the most incredible man I've ever known. But good sex is certainly a factor in that."

"Except that good sex is all Jason and I had," Penny reminded her. "Everything else was a lie."

"I'm not telling you to give the guy another chance," Paige said. "Only you can decide if you want to do that.

But I am going to remind you that there's more at stake now than just you and Jason."

She nodded. "Believe me, I'm thinking about the baby. I've hardly been able to think about anything else. But I didn't think that Jason might be worried, and I'm sorry you had to come all the way over here to check on me."

"I was planning on coming back anyway," her sister admitted. "I'm meeting with Blake in the morning to talk about the unveiling of the diamond."

Penny latched on to the change of topic gratefully. "Do you think that showcasing the diamond will be enough to turn things around for the McCords?"

"I know it will get customers in the door," Paige said. "After that, it's your designs that will do the rest."

"Speaking of designs, I have an engagement ring to work on in the morning, so I should get some sleep."

"Since I'm very excited to see what you come up with for that engagement ring, I'll let you." Paige kissed her cheek. "Sweet dreams, Penny."

But as she left her sister in the kitchen with the ice cream, Penny hoped she wouldn't dream at all. Because lately, all of her dreams seemed to focus on Jason.

Chapter Seven

Foley Industries had a corporate jet, and Jason had always felt that one of the biggest perks of being COO of the company was being able to avoid the usual headaches and hassles of commercial travel. Unfortunately, it was only one jet, and on rare occasions when it was in use elsewhere, he was forced to fly with a public carrier. First class, of course, but still…

His trip to Denver was one of those times. Thankfully, it wasn't a very long flight, and he had his BlackBerry and his laptop so he could work throughout the journey. Or at least pretend to work, while his thoughts were on Penny and the baby they were going to have.

Now that he was on his way home, he was anxious to see her, to plead his case in person and make plans for their future.

It took a few minutes before the baby's cries penetrated his thoughts, but once he became aware of them, nothing seemed to block them out.

He'd seen the mother in line at the check-in counter. She'd had a rolling suitcase in one hand, a three- or four-year-old child holding the other and a baby who couldn't have been more than a few months old in a sling across her chest. And he'd said a silent prayer of thanks that she wasn't waiting for the executive check-in.

But the curtain that separated first class from coach wasn't much of a sound barrier, and once he'd tuned into the baby's crying, he couldn't tune it out. In fact, after a few minutes it seemed to be growing louder, as if the baby was coming nearer.

Probably just his own impending parenthood playing games with his imagination, or so he thought, until the flight attendant moved briskly past him. He heard her, a few rows behind him, ask in a slightly impatient tone, "Can I help you?"

"My son needs to use the bathroom," a decidedly harried female voice replied.

"There are two lavatories at the rear of the plane," the attendant informed her, standing guard against any intrusion.

"I'm aware of that," the frazzled mother said through gritted teeth. "But they're both occupied, and a three-and-a-half year-old doesn't have fabulous bladder control, so unless you want to deal with that kind of mess, you'll please let me come through…"

With a resigned sigh, the attendant held back the curtain for the woman and her children to pass.

"Isn't there anything you can do to settle her down?" the flight attendant wanted to know.

Her question almost made Jason smile. The young woman clearly had even less experience with babies than he did, which was saying something. Because, aside from his niece, Olivia, who was now six years old, and whose diaper he'd changed exactly once way back when she was still wearing diapers, his experience was nonexistent.

"The switch is inside her diaper. As soon as I can get to it, I'll turn her off."

The flight attendant's mouth tightened, even as Jason's lips curved.

But the mother's troubles were not over, as she couldn't maneuver into the narrow bathroom with the baby.

"Mommy." The little boy's urgency was apparent.

She glanced around, anxiously searching for an answer to her dilemma. Most of the seats in executive class were occupied on this flight, and most of the occupants were busy with their laptops or their newspapers, or otherwise pretending they didn't even see the woman who had dared venture into their midst.

Her eyes locked on Jason's. He should have looked away, but she was obviously desperate and the flight attendant wasn't going to be any help, and while he wouldn't say he had a sudden paternal urge, he did hear himself say, "Do you need a hand?"

"Yeah. For just a minute. If you don't mind." And with that, she dropped the squawking red-faced baby in his lap and ducked into the bathroom behind the little boy.

"Well."

Jason looked down at the infant, who looked back at him with the biggest, bluest, tear-drenched eyes he had ever seen. Of course, the baby didn't respond to his comment. In fact, he guessed she didn't even hear it as she hadn't stopped screaming, except for the briefest fraction of a second and only then to draw more air into her lungs.

She squirmed, kicking her chubby little legs and flailing her pudgy arms and generally letting him know that she wasn't comfortable being held at arms' length on a stranger's knee. So Jason lifted her up against his shoulder, awkwardly patting her back with his free hand as he vaguely recalled having done with Olivia.

The baby stopped squirming, hiccuped twice, then let out an enormous belch, and spewed a gallon of something disgusting and smelly all over his suit jacket.

On the plus side, she did stop crying.

As much as Penny wanted to believe she could make her own decisions and figure out her plans, she didn't think it would hurt to talk to someone who had been in the same position she found herself in now.

Eleanor and Rex had returned late the night before, and Penny tracked her mother down in the library, where she was lounging on the sofa with a new book by her favorite author.

Eleanor looked up and, seeing her daughter hovering in the doorway, immediately put her book aside.

"How was your trip?" Penny asked.

"Fabulous," Eleanor said. "I've always loved San Francisco, and seeing a favorite city with someone you love…well, it just makes the experience even better."

"Where's Rex today?"

Her mother pouted. "He had to go to Houston for a meeting. Apparently being independently wealthy hasn't eradicated his desire to work every day—to feel useful, he says. Not that I really mind, it's just that after so many years apart, I don't want to miss out on another, single moment together."

Penny didn't know what to say to that. She had no experience with that type of all-consuming emotion, and circumstances being what they were, she wasn't likely to get any.

"But now you're here," Eleanor said, "which is just as good, because we haven't had a chance to chat, just the two of us, in a long time."

"I did want to talk to you," Penny admitted. "And then I wasn't sure if I should."

"Talk about Jason, you mean."

She nodded. "I know it must be awkward for you, since you're married to his father now."

"I was your mother first," Eleanor said. "And I'll always be your mother."

"It's a little strange, isn't it, that there was such distance between the two families for so long, and now you and Rex are married, Paige and Travis are engaged and I'm having Jason's baby."

"There have been a lot of big changes, but I'm happy that the feud is finally at an end."

Penny plucked at an imaginary thread on her sweater. "I'm worried that this…situation…with Jason and me might stir things up again."

"Don't," her mother said. "The situation with you and Jason has nothing to do with anyone but you and Jason. Although I am curious to know if you've decided what you're going to tell him when he gets back from Denver?"

"Tell him about what?"

"His proposal."

Penny frowned. "If you could call it a proposal. And how did you know about that anyway?"

"Rex, of course."

Penny should have guessed that Jason would tell his father, and that Jason's father would tell his wife. But when Penny and Jason had first gotten involved, there weren't so many family ties, and now she couldn't help but feel as if all the connections were tying her hands.

"So," Eleanor prompted, "are you going to say 'yes'?"

"No."

Her mother frowned, obviously disappointed.

"We're going to have a baby," Penny said gently. "But we were never really 'together'—you know Jason was only using me to get information on our search for the diamond."

Eleanor's frown deepened. "He may have had ulterior motives in the beginning, but I'm sure that once he got to know you, his intentions changed."

"Why are you sure of that? Because Rex said so?"

"Because the man who subjected himself to the wrath of two families by announcing your pregnancy at Thanksgiving dinner wouldn't have done so if he didn't intend to stick around for the fallout."

"I don't know what he intended," Penny admitted. "And even if he told me his intentions, how could I believe him? I was dating him for the better part of two months, and the whole time I honestly thought we had something special, that he cared. Now I know it was all a lie."

"I think he does care. And if you worked at building a life together, that caring would grow."

"I can't believe you're suggesting that I even think about marrying him," Penny said. "Especially after you spent thirty years trapped in a marriage to a man you didn't love."

"There's a big difference in the two situations."

"How do you figure that?"

"I was in love with someone else when I married your father," her mother reminded her gently.

"With Rex," Penny said.

Eleanor nodded. "I fell in love with him when I was sixteen years old and I never stopped loving him."

Penny was pleased that her mother had found happiness with her new husband, but there was still a question nagging at the back of her mind, one that had been there ever since she'd learned that Eleanor and Rex were teenage sweethearts finally reunited. "Did you never love Daddy?"

Her mother thought about the question for a long moment before answering.

"Devon had a lot of wonderful qualities," she finally said. "And I often thought that I might have fallen in love with him if I'd known him first. But later I was too busy resenting him for the circumstances that forced me into a marriage I didn't want and wasn't ready to appreciate the man that he was."

"And yet, you want to force me into a marriage with Jason."

Eleanor shook her head. "I don't want to force you into anything," she denied. "In fact, I want you to do what I didn't—to follow your heart."

Jason saw the mother from the plane again at baggage claim. Lindsay Conners she'd told him her name was, in the midst of her embarrassed and profuse apologies and offers to give him money for dry cleaning. Jason had declined, of course, simply removing the jacket and, folding it to cover the milky vomit, tucking it into his carry-on bag.

The baby was back in the sling over the mother's shoulder and, if not asleep, at least quiet. She found her suitcase and dragged it off of the luggage carousel, and when she turned, her eyes went wide, darting around the crowd of bodies and bags, frantically looking for something else. Or someone else, Jason realized, spotting the little boy over by the luggage carts where he'd set himself up with his coloring books and crayons.

In two quick strides, Jason was by her side, pointing her toward her son. "Over there."

"Oh, thank God." Her breath shuddered out, her eyes immediately filling with tears of gratitude and relief.

"Actually, my name's Jason," he told her.

She managed a laugh. "Thank you, Jason. I told him to stay put, but, well, I tell him a lot of things he doesn't seem to hear these days."

Jason lifted his bag off of the carousel and followed her over to where the little boy was coloring.

"Do you have kids?" she asked him.

"No," he said. "Not yet. But that will change in about six months."

"That would explain the I-want-to-help-but-don't-have-a-clue look on your face on the plane."

He winced. "Was I that transparent?"

"Yes, but you were still my savior," she told him.

"Any words of advice for a first-time dad-to-be?"

"Yeah, don't leave your wife at home with the kids

you claimed meant the world to you while you take off to Cozumel with your twenty-two-year-old secretary."

"I'm guessing it wasn't a business trip."

"The only business he ever thinks about these days is avoidance of family responsibilities. Now I'm scrambling to get back into the workplace after he urged me to give up my job to stay at home with the children." She sighed as she finished packing away the thick crayons. "I'm sorry. I didn't mean to go off on you. You just picked a bad time to be nice."

"I don't believe there's ever a bad time to be nice."

She managed to smile in response to that. "Well, thank you again for your help, Jason."

"Foley," he said. "Jason Foley."

"I thought you looked familiar," she said. "I used to work for your brother, Zane. It feels like a lifetime ago." She glanced pointedly at the little boy and then her baby. "Actually two lifetimes ago."

"How long did you work for Zane?"

"I was his executive assistant for four years. But like I said, it was a long time ago."

He handed her a business card. "When you get settled, give me a call."

"I appreciate the offer, Mr. Foley, but I don't need your charity."

"I'm not offering you charity, I'm offering you a job. You wouldn't have lasted four years as my brother's executive assistant if you couldn't manage people or handle pressure."

"Well, when you put it that way." She took the card. "I may be proud, but I'm not stupid."

That should have been the end of it, but Jason found

himself thinking about her long after he left the airport—or not Lindsay Conners so much as her situation. He didn't know how she managed on her own, or how Penny would manage on her own if she insisted on doing it that way. He knew that single mothers were hardly an anomaly in the current day and age, but he wondered why a woman would choose to go it alone if she didn't have to.

He could understand a wife booting her cheating husband to the curb, but he would never be unfaithful to the woman he chose to marry. He believed strongly in the sanctity of marriage and would neither commit nor forgive any infidelity. Of course, Penny didn't know him well enough to be sure of that, and recent revelations hadn't painted him in the most favorable light, but he figured he could prove himself over the next fifty or sixty years of their marriage.

Except that he still hadn't quite figured out how to get her to agree to the marriage.

When she left her mother in the library, Penny was feeling more confused than ever.

Follow her heart?

That's exactly what she'd thought she was doing when she made the decision to have her baby on her own. She didn't need a husband, and she sure as heck didn't need Jason Foley.

Except that Jason wanted to be a father to their baby, and she knew she couldn't refuse that. Still, there was a lot of ground between coparenting and cohabiting with legal ties.

But now even Paige was pressuring her to get back

together with Jason, so they could raise their child together. Of course, her sister was blissfully in love and wanted everyone else to be, too.

At least Blake seemed to be firmly ensconced in her corner, insisting that Penny shouldn't feel pressured to get married simply because she was pregnant. Of course, he had his own reasons for taking that position.

Only Tate had seemed neutral on the subject of her pregnancy. On the other hand, Penny hadn't really had an opportunity to talk to him about it, either.

But Penny wouldn't let herself be swayed by anyone else's thoughts and opinions. She already loved the child growing inside of her and would ultimately make a decision based on what was best for that child. And even though her relationship with Jason hadn't been everything she'd wanted it to be, she would never regret a single moment of the time she spent with him, because he had given her the greatest gift she could ever imagine in the baby growing inside her womb.

Jason was tired when he got home, and not particularly happy to find his father waiting in his living room.

"What are you doing here?"

"Your doorman let me in," Rex told him.

"I didn't mean my living room," he clarified. "I meant Houston."

"I had a meeting that went late, so I thought I would crash here tonight and drive back to Dallas in the morning."

Jason didn't mind his father dropping by or planning to stay. What he minded was the third degree he knew he was going to get.

"I brought a six-pack and ordered pizza," Rex said.

"I ate on the plane." But he went to the fridge, grabbed a bottle of beer he didn't particularly want and twisted off the cap. "Why are you really here, Dad? Because if it's to tell me that I screwed up, I don't need that pointed out to me."

"You did screw up," Rex agreed. "But you can still fix it."

"I'm working on it."

"Then you do plan to marry Penny?"

Jason took a long swallow from his bottle. "Yes," he said. "As soon as I can convince the bride."

"Then you should be busy planning a wedding, because I've seen you work impossible business deals, and I know that if you want this badly enough, you'll find a way to make it happen."

"Penny seems a little…resistant…to the idea."

Rex frowned, as if that possibility had never occurred to him. "She was happy enough to date you for the past couple of months. Why wouldn't she be jumping at the chance to marry you?"

"Maybe because she knows she was manipulated and she's determined not to be manipulated any longer."

"There's a difference between manipulation and finesse."

Jason set his half-empty bottle on the counter and scrubbed a hand over his jaw. "I'm not going to manipulate or finesse her into doing something she doesn't want to do."

"Then make her see that it's something she wants."

"I hope it is," he told his father. "But I had a lot of time to think while I was in Denver, and the one thing I realized is that no one has the right to decide what's right for Penny except Penny—not you, not her mother or her sister and especially not me."

"Well, I'll be damned," Rex said softly. "You have real feelings for her, don't you?"

Jason scowled. "Of course I have feelings for her."

"Do you love her?"

"Why do I have to put a label on my feelings?"

Rex shook his head. "I would have expected all of your experience with women to have taught you a few things."

"What things?" Jason asked warily.

"That women are romantics. They like candlelight dinners and flowers and wine—okay, maybe skip the wine because of the baby. But make an effort, show her how you feel, tell her how you feel. Women like words, too."

"I'm not going to lie to her."

"Of course not," his father agreed. "After all, lying's what got you into this mess."

Jason would have said that having unprotected sex was what had gotten him into this mess, but then he realized his father was right. The "mess" wasn't Penny's unexpected pregnancy but their separation, and Jason was determined to fix it.

Chapter Eight

"Penny, hi."

She heard the surprise in Jason's voice and knew he'd expected her to ignore the call, as she'd ignored so many of his calls and e-mails and text messages over the past few weeks.

"Hello, Jason."

"I just wanted to touch base to let you know that I'm back from Denver."

"Did you have a good trip?" she asked politely, because she'd promised herself she would make an effort to have a civil conversation with him. She was still hurt and angry, but she knew she had to get over those feelings if they were going to work together for the sake of their baby.

"It was successful, at least from a business standpoint," he told her. "But it took longer than I expected, so now I have to go in to the office tomorrow."

"I work in retail," she reminded him. "I have no sympathy for anyone who complains about having to work an occasional Saturday."

"Are you working tomorrow?" he asked her.

"No," she admitted.

"Good, because I should be finished at the office by noon and I thought I might make the trip into Dallas after that, so that we could talk."

"Actually, I have plans for tomorrow," she told him.

"Oh." He managed to express both disappointment and skepticism in the single syllable.

She couldn't blame him for being skeptical, not after the way she'd been dodging him over the past several weeks. But she did have legitimate plans this time, as she explained, "Someone was considerate enough to give me a spa day, and I've booked it for tomorrow."

"Then I guess I shouldn't complain," he said.

"And I should say 'thank you'."

"You thought it was considerate, huh?"

She'd thought it was thoughtful and sweet, and she still remembered the note he sent via e-mail to her. The subject line had read simply *SPA-tacular,* and Penny had nearly deleted the message, assuming it was an unsolicited advertisement. Then she recognized Jason's e-mail address and curiosity had prompted her to read further.

Please contact Gina at SPA-tacular to schedule a day of pampering for yourself and a friend. My treat. Because I know I've been the cause of far too much stress in your life recently.

Enjoy,

Jason

"I did think it was considerate," she said now. "But that doesn't mean I forgive you."

"I know. And I don't blame you. I just wish—"

"Don't."

"Don't what?"

"Don't push," she said. "Let's just both be satisfied that we've managed to have a fairly civil conversation tonight."

"Okay," he agreed. "I won't push. But what would you say if I invited you to go for dinner tomorrow night after your spa day?"

"I'd say you were pushing."

"I take it that's a no?"

"That's a no," she confirmed.

"Then I'll say good night now, and maybe I'll talk to you tomorrow."

"Maybe," she agreed, but she was smiling a little when she said it.

Penny had never felt so pampered.

She knew what Jason was doing—softening her up so that she would be more amenable to his plans, which apparently included getting married so they could raise their baby together. And at the moment, she definitely felt like she was softening. She'd been buffed and polished and massaged and oiled so that her skin was like silk and her muscles were completely lax. But while she was definitely feeling appreciative of his efforts, she still had no intention of giving up her dreams and settling for a marriage of convenience.

"It's occurred to me," Paige said, lounging in a cushy leather chair identical to her sister's as they waited for the polish on their toenails to dry, "that maybe I was wrong about Jason."

Penny's brows lifted. "Or maybe being slathered in warm mud made you mellow."

"Maybe," Paige agreed. "I did like the mud. And the massage. But you have to give the guy points for thinking of it. I mean, what woman wouldn't want a man who is willing to pamper her like this?"

"*This* woman," Penny said firmly. "Because he didn't do it to be thoughtful and generous, although he can be both. He did it to score points."

Her sister raised her arms over her head. "Touchdown."

Penny picked up her glass of mineral water, sipped. "You're so juvenile."

"Youthful," Paige corrected, with a saucy grin.

"Juvenile," Penny said again.

Her twin stuck out her tongue, then she asked, "Have you given any more thought to his proposal?"

"How can you think I would even consider it, after everything he did?"

Paige was silent for a minute, no doubt remembering how furious and indignant she'd been when she'd learned about Jason's plans—and she wasn't the one he'd been sleeping with.

"Okay, I can understand why you'd be reluctant," she allowed.

"I'm not reluctant, I'm firmly opposed."

"Then you're stronger and braver than I am, because I'd find the idea of having a baby on my own a little daunting."

"Believe me, I'm daunted," Penny told her sister.

"I'm just not convinced that getting married for the sake of a baby would be anything less than a disaster."

"If the baby was the only reason you were getting married," Paige agreed. "But you and Jason had something good going. You were happy with him."

"I was oblivious."

"You were in love."

"I think my toes are dry," Penny said.

Paige reached over and covered her hand so that she couldn't get up and flee. "I know you, Penny. And you never would have slept with him unless you had pretty strong feelings for him. Those feelings don't just disappear because you want them to."

"I want *him* to disappear," she grumbled.

"I don't see that happening, either," her sister warned.

"I want…" Penny sighed, then finally admitted, "I want what you have with Travis."

"Why do you think you can't have that with Jason?"

"Because he doesn't love me."

"Did he say that he doesn't?"

"No, but he didn't say that he did, either."

"And even if he did, you wouldn't trust his motives at this point," Paige guessed.

She nodded.

"Well, no one would disagree that you have reason to be wary. On the other hand, without risk there is no reward."

But for Penny's bruised and battered heart, the risks were just too great.

When Jason went into work Saturday morning, his secretary was already at her desk. Since Barb rarely worked overtime and never worked weekends, he couldn't help but wonder why she was there.

"Coffee's on in your office, there's a fax on your desk from EDI Drilling and a pile of correspondence to be reviewed and signed so that I can get it into the mail before the post office closes today."

"Thank you," he said cautiously.

But his surprise must have been evident, because she said, "You can thank me with a bonus in my next paycheck."

Jason made a mental note to do that.

First things first, though. He poured himself a cup of coffee and glanced at the fax. It wasn't anything urgent, so he set it aside and directed his attention to the correspondence.

An hour later, he took the stack of letters out to Barb's desk. She was busy at the computer, and he took a moment to glance around at the assortment of photos that were taped around her work station. It was like a family history in pictures.

In a place of honor beside her computer was the photo of Barb and her husband, Ted, on their thirty-fifth wedding anniversary. Then there were photos of each of the three sons they had together: the eldest with his wife on their wedding day; the middle one in his military uniform; and the youngest in his cap and gown at his college graduation. Then there were the photos—at least half a dozen—of her new grandbaby.

Jason had no photos on his desk. Of course, there were no macaroni pencil holders or floppy stuffed elephants hanging over his computer monitor, either.

But as he moved closer to drop the papers on her

desk, he found his gaze again drawn to the anniversary photo.

"Thirty-five years," he mused, realizing—probably for the first time—that his secretary had been married for more years than he'd been alive.

Though Barb looked up from her computer screen, her fingers never stopped moving on the keys. "Did you say something, Mr. Foley?"

"I was just remarking on the fact that you've been married thirty-five years."

Her eyes moved automatically to the photo and her lips curved. "Actually, it's almost thirty-eight now."

Thirty-eight. His dad and his mom had barely shared half that number of years together before she died. He'd never known anyone who had been married—and apparently happily—for so long.

"Thirty-eight years ago, when you were exchanging your vows, did you know it would last?"

She stopped typing and swiveled in her chair to give him her full attention. "Of course," she said, then chuckled. "But I was nineteen years old and incredibly naive. I had no idea how hard it would be at times to make our marriage work.

"Had I known then what I know now…" She shook her head. "Let's just say I probably wouldn't have been so eager to rush down the aisle. On the other hand, I also wouldn't give up a single day that we've had together. I couldn't imagine my life without him."

"You're lucky," he said, "that your marriage succeeded when so many fail these days."

"Lucky?" The scorn in her voice left him in no doubt as to her opinion about that. "Luck has nothing to do with it. It's hard work and commitment that get you through the tough times. The reason so many marriages fail is that young people nowadays don't know what it means to stick it out through the tough times."

He was no stranger to hard work or commitment, and if he managed to convince Penny to marry him, he would stick it out. He had never walked away from his responsibilities and he sure as heck wouldn't walk away from his child.

"Why the sudden interest in my marriage?" Barb's gaze narrowed. "Did you meet a special lady who has you thinking about forever?"

Jason wasn't in the habit of talking to his secretary about his private life. In fact, he wasn't in the habit of talking to anyone about his private life. On the other hand, it seemed as if everyone had an opinion these days on what he should do—and a vested interested in his plans. It would be interesting to get the opinion of someone who had nothing to gain, and Barb was nothing if not discreet.

"Someone very special," he said, because that part, at least, was true.

"And you love her?" she prompted.

Jason hesitated, and she huffed out an impatient breath.

"If you have to think about that, then you have no business thinking about marriage.

"Hard work and commitment may be the building blocks of a solid marriage, but love is the mortar that holds it all together. Without love, any wind of discontent or distrust—and believe me, there will be storms—will have the blocks tumbling down."

It was hard to argue with thirty-eight-years' experience, but Jason wasn't discouraged. Because he would love the baby, and he knew Penny would love the baby, and he just had to trust that would be enough. Because he wouldn't risk anything more.

Penny called Jason when she got home from her spa day with Paige. It was the first time since their breakup that she'd initiated contact, and she was more than a little nervous about doing so. Especially when he didn't immediately answer.

Not that she'd expected he would be waiting by the phone, but she was a little disappointed that he didn't seem to be home. And then she wondered, it being a Saturday night, if he had a date.

The thought came to her out of the blue, but it wasn't an unreasonable one. Yeah, he'd proposed to her, but only because he knew she was carrying his baby. In reality, they'd broken up weeks before, and there was no reason that he couldn't be dating someone else by now.

Just when Penny had resigned herself to leaving a message—or not leaving one—he picked up.

"Hello?"

"Oh, uh, hi. Jason. It's Penny."

"I recognized your voice," he said, and sounded pleased to hear from her. "How was your spa day?"

"Fabulous," she said. "Actually, one of the reasons I was calling was to thank you."

"You already thanked me."

"Not as profusely as I would have if I'd known how truly wonderful the experience was going to be."

"Did your sister enjoy it, too?"

"So much that she's ready to join the Jason Foley fan club."

"I have a fan club?"

She laughed. "Not really, no. At least not that I'm aware of."

"Well, you're welcome anyway. But you said that was one of your reasons for calling."

"Yeah. I also wanted to let you know that I have a doctor's appointment Tuesday."

"Is something wrong? Are you feeling okay?"

"Nothing's wrong," she assured him. "I'm fine. It's just a checkup."

"Oh. Okay. What time is it?"

"Two o'clock."

"Are you just keeping me informed, or are you asking me to go with you?"

She knew he expected her to balk, and maybe there was a part of her that wanted to, that wanted to keep this baby all to herself. But she knew that wouldn't be fair, that this was too important for her to shut him out.

"That's up to you," she said.

"I'll pick you up at the store," he told her.

"I can meet you—"

"I'll pick you up," he repeated.

She sighed. "You're pushing again."

"I'm being environmentally conscious—saving you gas, since we're both going in the same direction," he countered.

"You have an answer for everything, don't you?"

"Not yet," he said. "But I'm working on it."

And that was precisely why she was worried.

* * *

When Jason arrived at McCord Jewelers Tuesday afternoon, the first thing he noticed was that the Santa Magdalena Diamond had been given a place of honor at the center of the showroom floor. Set atop a pedestal inside a glass case and spotlighted, it was shown to full advantage. Certainly, anyone gazing upon the gem would be attracted by its beauty, and alarmed to learn of its history.

Originally mined in India, the Santa Magdalena Diamond had apparently caused misfortune to everyone who had ever owned it, so maybe it wasn't so surprising that Paige and Travis had decided to donate the diamond to the Smithsonian rather than risk being subjected to its reputed curse. But using it on an interim basis to generate traffic through the store was another brilliant idea. And apparently a successful one, as the sales staff were all busy with customers, while still others were avidly browsing.

"It seems busy for a Tuesday afternoon," he commented to Penny when she joined him.

"Business has been good. Partly, it's the season— we're always busy between Thanksgiving and Christmas. But busier this year, I think, because of the diamond. We haven't had a quiet moment in the store since it was put on display."

"That was the point, wasn't it?"

"Yes, as much as I'm sure it disappoints you, the McCord fortunes seem to be turning around."

"Believe it or not, I'm not disappointed at all," he told her.

Penny didn't know what to believe, especially when

she herself had mixed feelings about the gem. She was happy it had been found, grateful it was helping to resolve the family's financial woes, and still a little resentful that it had meant so much to Jason that he'd used her to try to get information about the search for it.

The Santa Magdalena Diamond was a status symbol to him, and finding it—especially if he'd been able find it before the McCords did—would have been quite the coup. There were times she couldn't help but wonder if he thought of their baby in the same way. If it was all about the acquisition to him. And if, as soon as she gave in to his demands, he wouldn't want her or their child anymore.

"And in case you didn't hear," he continued, "the Foley-McCord feud is over."

Jason's comment snapped her out of her reverie.

"I thought that was just a rumor," she said lightly.

"You don't believe it?"

"I'm reserving judgment."

"In that case, I will do everything I can to prove it to you."

Penny knew he would, and what worried her was how much she already wanted to believe him.

The doctor's surprise upon seeing Jason come into the examining room with Penny was obvious.

"I'm Jason Foley," he said, introducing himself before Penny could—or maybe because he suspected that Penny wouldn't. "The baby's father."

Dr. Brennan looked askance at the mother-to-be. Apparently, she remembered Penny telling her that the baby's father wasn't around and wouldn't be involved in the pregnancy or birth. Which had obviously been wishful thinking on her part.

She put her regrets aside as the doctor went through the usual checkup routine, including the measuring of her blood pressure and her weight. Penny kicked off her shoes before stepping on the scale, as if that would make a difference. And while the doctor didn't comment on her action, her raised brows told Penny that it hadn't gone unnoticed.

After noting an additional three-pound gain on her chart, Dr. Brennan excused herself for a moment. That wasn't a usual part of the routine, which of course made Penny wonder about it.

"We usually do an ultrasound at twenty weeks," the doctor told Penny and Jason when she returned. "But we have a room and a machine available, so I'd like to take a look at your baby today."

Penny swallowed. "You think something's wrong with the baby?"

Jason moved closer and took her hand.

For a minute, she'd almost forgotten he was there. But now she was glad of his presence and his support. If there was something wrong, if she'd done something—

"I don't think anything's wrong," the doctor's assurance interrupted her panicked thoughts. "But I have some questions that an ultrasound may be able to answer."

"Can I stay for the test?" Jason asked.

"As long as it's okay with Penny," Dr. Brennan said.

Making it impossible for Penny to refuse.

But she really was grateful he was there with her. The doctor didn't seem overly concerned, but she'd probably done hundreds of ultrasounds and delivered hundreds of babies. This was Penny's first, and she was terrified. She'd been doing everything the doctor and the pregnancy books said—okay, ice cream intake excluded—but what if she'd done something wrong before she knew she was pregnant? What if she was somehow responsible for harming their baby?

As if cognizant of her thoughts, Jason squeezed her hand reassuringly as they followed the doctor to another room.

The bed had been prepped and Penny was given a sheet to cover up her lower body.

"Do you want me to wait outside?" Jason asked.

"You're not going to see anything you haven't seen before," she reminded him, even as she wished she could forget that he'd seen it all as recently as a week and a half earlier.

She wriggled out of her skirt and draped it neatly over the back of the chair. Then she hopped up on the bed and unfolded the sheet she'd been given. All the while, Jason pretended to be engrossed in a series of posters depicting the stages of a baby's development through pregnancy. Or maybe he wasn't pretending. Maybe he really was interested in what their baby looked like right now.

When the doctor came back in, she took the chair near the bed and directed Jason to stand on the other side, so that he could see the image that would be visible on the screen. Then she folded down the sheet and squirted some warm gel on Penny's tummy, spreading it around with a plastic probe—a transducer she called it, and explained that it transmitted the echoes of the sound waves into a picture on the monitor.

"Well, that explains it," Dr. Brennan said.

"What?" Penny stared at the screen but couldn't really decipher anything other than a dark, elongated oval with two lighter colored shapes inside.

Two?

She blinked.

Maybe the doctor's equipment was out of whack. That was the only explanation she could think of for there to be two images, almost like mirrors of one another. Unless—

Dr. Brennan smiled. "You're going to have twins."

Penny stared at the monitor, but she refused to believe what she could see with her own eyes. She'd barely had a chance to adjust to the idea of one baby and now the doctor was suggesting there were *two* babies?

"What do you mean? How can there be twins?"

Dr. Brennan pointed at the screen. "As you can clearly see, there are two babies in there. And the presence of those two babies explains your excessive tiredness and unusual weight gain."

"I can't have two babies," Penny protested. "I don't know what to do with one."

"That's a common concern of first-time mothers who learn they're carrying twins," the doctor said, as if that might reassure her. "Having a baby requires some major lifestyle changes, so having two babies requires even more.

"But you're fortunate," Dr. Brennan continued, "in that you have an interested partner willing to share both the joys and trials of pregnancy and parenthood with you."

Penny managed a weak smile, though she thought the doctor was being rather presumptuous considering that Jason had, so far, been present at one appointment.

A thought which made her realize that Jason hadn't said a single word since he'd come into the room, and she wondered if he was feeling as shell-shocked as she was. But when she glanced over at him, she saw that he didn't look stunned or panicked, he looked…awed. As if he had never seen anything more amazing than the sight of those two tiny little hearts beating on the screen. And in that moment, something inside her own heart softened.

Chapter Nine

When Jason suggested picking up something for dinner, Penny didn't object. Of course, he probably could have suggested they go straight to the airport and catch the next flight to Vegas and she would have nodded, still with that deer-in-the-headlights look in her eyes. And he couldn't deny that the thought did cross his mind, but he'd meant what he'd said to his father. He didn't want to manipulate her, and that's what it would be if he took advantage of her current state of shock to pursue his own agenda.

He stopped at the supermarket near his condo to pick up a few groceries, and it was only when he parked the car that Penny seemed to register where they were. She got out when he did and followed him into the store. He grabbed a basket and started toward the produce section. He picked out some red and yellow peppers, a head of broccoli, a bunch of carrots, a zucchini, some spring onions and a handful of shiitake mushrooms. Penny didn't say a word, even though he knew broccoli wasn't one of her favorite vegetables.

He led the way toward meat and poultry, where he picked out a nice lean steak, because the doctor had said that red meat was a good source of iron. Again, Penny followed wordlessly behind him. Her unusual silence was really starting to worry him, so when they cut down the aisle with baby essentials on their way to the check-out and they were walking past a tower of diapers, Jason couldn't resist teasing, "Think we should start stocking up on those now?"

And Penny burst into tears.

He put the basket down in the middle of the floor and pulled her into his arms. She came willingly, burying her face in his shoulder to muffle her sobs.

If he was surprised that she turned to him rather than away, he didn't waste too much time thinking about it. He was too busy enjoying the feel of her soft curves pressed against him. He rubbed her back gently, murmured reassuringly, although he wasn't exactly sure what he was reassuring her about.

After a few minutes—and more than a few curious glances from passers by—the flood of tears had reduced to a trickle.

She said something then, but her words were muffled against his shirt. So he dipped his head toward her and, inhaling the familiar fresh citrus scent of her shampoo, realized it was just one of the many things he'd missed about her.

"What did you say?" he asked gently.

She drew back, just a little. "I said, I d-don't even know how t-to change a d-diaper."

"Well, we've got some time to figure that out."

"I d-don't know how t-to do anything."

"We'll figure it all out," he said. "Everything will be okay."

She tipped her head back to look up at him. Her green eyes were red-rimmed and shimmering with tears, her nose was red, and her cheeks were streaked, but she was still beautiful. And still wary. "How do you know?"

"Because we're going to take it one step at a time," he told her. "Together."

After her meltdown in the middle of the grocery store, Penny just wanted to go home and hide under the covers of her bed forever—or at least until after her baby was born.

Babies, she mentally amended, and nearly melted down again.

Clearly, her pregnancy hormones were out of control, and while hiding under the covers still seemed like a good idea, she knew that she had to talk to Jason first. But not until after dinner. She tended to avoid confrontation at the best of times, and an empty stomach was definitely not the best of times.

Even though Jason ate out so often during office hours—whether with business associates or just grabbing a bite on the run—he'd learned to cook so that he could enjoy a homemade meal every once in a while. Penny used to think she was a decent cook, but his abilities in the kitchen put her efforts to shame. And even after a long day at the office, he never complained about putting in some extra time in the kitchen. And his cooking was one of the perks she'd enjoyed while they were dating.

While Jason chopped and diced, Penny sat back and watched. His movements were easy and sure, and without a cookbook in sight. When the veggies were prepared, he dumped them into a large glass bowl and set it aside. A new knife, a new cutting board and the steak was cut into long thin slices.

Watching him reminded her of being at one of those Japanese restaurants where the chef does all the cooking in front of the customers. Except that she'd been intimately involved with this chef, and watching Jason's hands chop and mix and stir with such effortless mastery brought to mind memories of those hands moving with the same effortless mastery over all the erogenous zones of her body.

He drizzled olive oil into the deep frying pan, then tossed in the garlic cloves he'd crushed, and the sizzle and scent made her mouth water. Or maybe it was the delicious man in front of the stove who really made her mouth water.

"What are you thinking?" Jason asked her.

She couldn't very well tell him the truth, so she went for the next thought that popped into her mind.

"I was thinking that two babies mean I have twice as many reasons to be terrified." And it was absolutely true, even if it hadn't been what she was thinking in the moment.

"I thought I was the only one who was scared."

She stole a slice of pepper from the bowl while he wasn't looking. "And I didn't think anything scared you."

"Neither did I, until you told me that you were pregnant."

"You didn't show any signs of panic."

He shrugged as he stirred the meat. "I wouldn't be a very effective negotiator in the boardroom if I didn't know how to hide my feelings."

"And your motives." The words were out before she could stop them, or maybe she didn't even try.

"You're right," he admitted. "Although I'm usually more forthright in my personal life than in my business dealings, the line got a little blurred when we were together."

"For you, maybe. I didn't even know there was a line."

"I think we're getting a little off-topic here." He dumped the veggies into the pan, added the stir-fry sauce he'd already whisked together—again without a recipe.

"You're right. I'm sorry. But I honestly don't see how we can come to any agreement about anything when I can't trust that you mean what you say."

"I never told you anything that wasn't true," he told her.

"You just never told me the whole truth."

"I'm telling you the whole truth now. I want to be with you, Penny, and to be a father to our babies."

He dished up the stir-fry, setting one bowl in front of Penny and one on the other side of the table. She picked up her fork, though she suddenly wasn't feeling very hungry.

"I also think," Jason continued, "that two babies need two parents on hand."

She wasn't fooled by his easy tone—she wasn't going to be fooled by anything he said again. So she didn't want to admit that she was feeling more than a little unnerved by the thought of handling twins on her own, especially remembering that her mother had often said two babies were about ten times as much work as one. On the other hand, her meltdown in the supermarket had probably given him at least a hint of her feelings.

"Maybe I could hire a nanny," she suggested.

He sighed. "You're right. There are other options. But I want to be involved, Penny. Let me help. Please."

Maybe it was that he'd asked instead of demanded. Maybe it was just that she was feeling more than a little panicked. But whatever the reason, she found herself actually considering his offer.

"Okay," she finally said. "*You* can hire the nanny. You can more easily afford it, anyway."

"I don't want to hire someone." He stabbed a piece of steak with his fork. "I want to marry you."

She shook her head, but not as vigorously as she might have three days—or even three hours—earlier. "Don't you think a wedding would cause more problems than it solves?" she asked him.

"No, I don't," he replied, and sounded as if he really meant it.

She pushed her empty bowl away. Obviously, she'd been hungrier than she'd realized, or the babies were, anyway. And just thinking *babies* nearly sent her into a tailspin again.

"Are you proposing a business relationship or a personal one?"

"What do you want?"

"I want to go back five months and take a cab home from Missy Harcourt's wedding."

"I screwed up, Penny. I know that. But I can honestly say that I don't regret a single moment that I spent with you."

"Even though you didn't get the information you needed to find the Santa Magdalena Diamond first?"

"Maybe I wasn't honest with you at the beginning, but the truth is, what happened between us stopped being about the diamond long before I ever took you to my bed."

She didn't believe him. Because if she did, she might let herself hope that their relationship actually meant something to him. And if she started to believe that, then she might be willing to open up her heart to him again. And that was something she couldn't let happen.

She didn't want to marry him, and yet… "I don't want to deprive my babies of a father."

"I'll be there for them," Jason assured her. "And for you, however and whenever you need me."

She took a deep breath. "Well, it's starting to look like I might need a husband."

Husband.

The word echoed in Jason's mind.

"Are you saying…that you'll marry me?"

She nodded. "It seems like the most reasonable thing to do, under the circumstances."

He shouldn't complain about the reason when it was getting him what he wanted, but it didn't seem like an enthusiastic endorsement for marriage. But he knew she was still shaken by the revelation that she was carrying twins, and despite his earlier assertion that he wouldn't use that info to sway her, he wasn't going to try to talk her out of it, either.

"How's Friday?" he asked.

"For what?"

"The wedding."

She blinked. "*This* Friday?"

"Why not?"

She was silent for a moment, as if trying to think of a reason, but in the end, she only shrugged. "I guess if we're going to do it, there's no reason to wait."

Unfortunately she was only talking about marriage and not any one of the numerous other things he wanted to do with her. He pushed the thought aside, to focus on more immediate matters.

"Is Vegas okay, or did you want to go to one of the islands?"

"I was thinking city hall," she admitted.

"We'll go with Vegas," he decided. "Then we don't have to worry about any waiting periods."

"How did we go from a doctor's appointment to dinner to a wedding date?" she wondered aloud.

Jason felt a slight twinge of guilt but reminded himself that the ends justified the means. Maybe they hadn't planned this pregnancy, but he wouldn't ever be sorry, because the babies she carried had given him the second chance he hadn't even known he wanted.

Now it was up to him to make the most of it.

But Penny started to doubt her decision almost as soon as Jason dropped her off at home. By the time Friday morning came around, she was still wavering. Was she really going to do this? What had changed her mind? Was she foolish enough to hope that a marriage of convenience could lead to real, long-lasting happiness?

Because she wasn't sure of the answers to any of those questions, she didn't advise anyone of her plans. Instead, she told Paige that she was going to work from home on Friday, finishing up some design work. And she waited until her mother had gone out to run some errands, then left a note in the library for her, saying only that she would be away for the weekend.

She still wasn't sure she would go through with the wedding.

But her bag was packed and her passport was in her purse, so she played around with some sketches while she waited for him to show up. That way her working-from-home story wasn't really a lie, and she wasn't watching the clock and worrying that Jason might have changed *his* mind.

But as she finished up the sketch of a bracelet to be made of twisted strands of copper studded with numerous gems, she worried about her deception. She'd never had secrets from her sister before. Not until she started dating Jason the first time, and now she'd fallen back into the same pattern. Then again, Paige had obviously been keeping secrets from her, most notably her search for the Santa Magdalena Diamond and her romance with Travis Foley.

The knock at the door had her pencil slipping from her fingers, then JoBeth peeked into the room and announced that Penny had a guest. Her tone of disapproval revealed Jason's identity more clearly than if she'd announced his name. She'd been Devon McCord's housekeeper for more than thirty years, and his dislike of all things Foley had apparently seeped into her blood. Which made Penny wonder how Rex—now married to Devon's widower and living in the McCord mansion— was settling in. But she didn't wonder long, having her own greater worries at the moment.

And one of those worries was that she still didn't know what she should do. But she grabbed her bag, pointedly ignored the housekeeper's raised eyebrows and went to meet Jason.

He was waiting in the foyer, and her heart gave one of those funny little bumps against her ribs, proving that whatever else she felt, she was still attracted to him. As for the rest of those feelings, well, if he was willing to marry her and be a father to their babies, why wouldn't she say yes and figure it out later?

"Are you ready?" Jason asked.

"I'm ready," she said, and hoped it was true.

Penny always thought she'd like to visit Vegas. Everything she'd seen of the city on television shows or in the movies was glamorous and exciting, but as the private plane began its descent, her stomach was a mass of knots and nerves.

Again, Jason seemed to be attuned to her mood and her concerns, as he reached over to take her hand, linking their fingers together.

"We're doing the right thing," he said.

She nodded, though she wasn't entirely convinced.

"I'll do my best to be a good father to our babies," he told her.

She just nodded.

"And I'll do my best to be a good husband, too."

"We're getting married for the babies," she said. "I don't want or expect it to mean anything more than that."

"I can't blame you for being wary," he said. "But I hope that in time you'll learn to trust me again."

"Speaking of time," she said, because she didn't want

to talk about their past and she dared not look too far into the future, "how soon can we get married?"

His smile was wry. "I'd like to think you're anxious to wear my ring, but I'm guessing you just want it over and done with."

"Ring?" She felt a tiny surge of panic. "I didn't even think about the rings."

"Don't worry," he said. "It's taken care of."

And he pulled a box out of his pocket to prove it. The lavender color of the packaging was unmistakably McCord's, so she had to give him credit for both tact and taste. But when he opened the lid, she was stunned.

It was a three-carat, brilliant-cut canary diamond set in a wide band that had been formed by forging together eight narrow ribbons of yellow gold, symbolizing the linking of two hands together.

"Where did you get that?"

"At McCord's, of course." He smiled. "Did you really think I would dare shop for your ring anywhere else?"

"But why that ring?"

His smile faltered. "You don't like it?"

"I'm just…surprised. It's not a traditional design."

"Maybe that's why it appealed to me. Because nothing about our relationship has been traditional." But something in her voice must have clued him in, because he said, "It's one of yours, isn't it?"

She nodded. "You really didn't know?"

"I didn't think about it," he admitted. "But now that I do, I should have guessed."

It wasn't just one of her designs, but designed while she was dating Jason and inspired by her relationship with him—not that she was going to admit as much.

"I'm guessing, then, that you like it?" he prompted.

"It's one of my favorite pieces," she said. "But…what about your ring? Or didn't you—"

He handed her another lavender box. Inside it was a masculine version of the same design—a little bit wider and heavier, and minus the diamond, but clearly designed to match, like two parts of a whole.

As they were going to be two parts joined together when they exchanged the rings.

The thought sent funny little quivers through her belly, more excitement than apprehension now. Or maybe it was just the plane touching down.

Penny was in awe as they drove down the strip toward their hotel. It was so much bigger and brighter, more than she'd imagined.

"Where are we getting married?" she asked Jason.

"We're scheduled for a two o'clock ceremony in the Starlight Chapel."

She tore her gaze away from the window. "You booked a ceremony?"

"Is that a problem?"

"No," she said, though she was surprised that he'd obviously paid a lot more attention to all the little details of their wedding than she had. "I just figured we'd find some little chapel on the strip and have a quick ceremony officiated by a second-rate Elvis impersonator."

"Just because it's Vegas doesn't mean it has to be tacky."

"I'm beginning to realize that."

"You've never been to Vegas before," he guessed.

She shook her head. "It's nothing like I expected. I mean, the strip is exactly what you see in all the movies and on television, but there's so much more than just the neon lights and flashy cars.

"Oh," she exclaimed, as something else caught her eye. "The Venetian."

The name was barely more than a reverent whisper, as her hand lifted to the window, as if she could reach through it and touch the majestic hotel.

"Is it true that you can actually ride a gondola and eat in St. Mark's Square inside?"

"It's true," he assured her. "And it is pretty spectacular, but on a much smaller scale than Venice itself."

"I've never been to Italy, either," she admitted.

He frowned at that. "Don't you have family in Italy?"

"Gabby's mother is Italian," she confirmed. "And she invited Paige and me to go over for a visit the summer we were sixteen, but my dad wouldn't allow it."

"Why not?"

"Because Gabby's beauty and celebrity had already put her in the spotlight and he worried that she would be a negative influence on us."

The more Jason knew about Devon McCord, the more he agreed that the man had been a selfish sonofabitch. While he kept his wife and children safely ensconced at home, he was traveling the world and frittering away their fortune. No wonder Penny had been so eager for a little attention and excitement, so eager to experience life.

"Vegas isn't Italy," he said again. "But we'll take a few days and I'll show you around."

"Really?" She seemed surprised—and unexpectedly pleased—by his offer.

"Sure," he said. "Although a few days isn't really long

enough to see and do everything, it will at least give you a preview of what you might want to see on another visit."

"I think I'd like to come back sometime," she admitted.

"How about for our first anniversary?"

"That would be nice," she said, but the light in her eyes faded and he inwardly cursed himself for mentioning their impending marriage, because now she was thinking about the reasons for it. And he knew it wasn't the babies she carried that dimmed the spark of excitement, but her distrust of him. He'd done that to her, taken her innocence, destroyed her naïveté.

He would give anything to go back in time and tell her the truth before she heard it from her sister, because the whole truth was more than Paige had known. The truth was, he'd grown to care a great deal for Penny— more than he was even ready to admit to himself.

Jason had made reservations at the Celestial Resort and Casino, and after he'd taken care of the check-in, they rode up to the thirty-fifth floor—just the two of them, a bellboy with their bags and the elevator attendant, in an elevator that could easily hold fifty people and was as lavishly decorated as everything else she'd seen in the short walk through the lobby.

Their hotel suite was even more spectacular.

Penny was a McCord, so she was hardly a stranger to wealth or extravagance, but she had never seen anything that compared to the stunning opulence of the rooms.

Jason tipped the bellboy and sent him on his way while Penny checked out the view from the wall of floor-to-ceiling windows, and found herself looking down at a lake-size swimming pool.

"They don't do anything by half measures here, do they?"

"Not at any of the places I'll be taking you," he assured her.

"I have to admit, whenever I thought about getting married someday, I never thought it would happen like this," she told him.

"In Vegas?"

She managed to smile. "Actually, I'm okay with the Vegas part. It's the whole getting-married-because-I'm-pregnant-and-too-damn-scared-to-go-it-alone part that's bothering me. And the why-am-I-doing-this-when-I-know-he's-going-to-wake-up-one-morning-and-realize-he's-trapped-in-a-life-he-never-wanted part."

"This wasn't what either of us planned, obviously, but I'm not unhappy about the babies or our marriage."

"You're not?"

"It wasn't as if I never planned to get married and have a family someday, I just hadn't yet gotten to that part of my plans."

"Really?"

"I'm a thirty-two-year-old, financially secure man with a stable job, so I don't have any concerns about what this marriage means for me."

"You have concerns about me?"

He shrugged. "You're only twenty-six and you've led a fairly sheltered life. After today, you're going to be a wife, and in less than six months the mother of two babies."

"Are you trying to get me to change my mind about this?"

"No," he said, then paused. "But maybe I'm a little worried that I pushed you too quickly in this direction."

He sounded as if he meant it, as if he really was concerned about her wants and her needs, and the knowledge stirred feelings she'd been trying to ignore.

"I know how to push back," she assured him.

He studied her for a long moment, and finally nodded. "In that case, we'd better get ready for the wedding."

As much as she thought she was ready, Penny experienced another moment of uncertainty when the ceremony began. Standing beside Jason and listening to the dark-suited minister recite the traditional words, she felt a pang of regret that this wasn't, except in the most technical sense, a real wedding.

She'd never been a gambler, but this was Vegas, and she knew she was taking a very big gamble in agreeing to marry Jason. But despite her nerves and apprehension, she wasn't going into it against her will. Even knowing what he'd done and why he'd done it, she wanted to marry him. She wanted to be with him, to raise her babies with him, to build a family together.

She wanted him to love her as much as she loved him.

There. She'd admitted it. She was in love with Jason Foley. Maybe she was stupid, maybe she was naive, maybe she was setting herself up to have her heart broken again—she didn't know. She only knew she could no longer deny her feelings.

Follow your heart, her mother had said, and that was what she intended to do.

Maybe it was a gamble, but she was ready to ante up. Because she was in love with the man she was going to marry and she was betting everything she had on a long and happy future together.

She'd felt a twinge of regret as she walked toward the front of the chapel past the empty chairs that lined the aisle. Whenever she'd let herself dream of her wedding day, she'd always envisioned her family celebrating the occasion with her. But she'd deliberately kept silent about her plans to marry Jason, not just because she hadn't been certain it would happen but because she was even less certain of their support.

Then she'd looked up and met Jason's gaze, and the easy warmth and obvious appreciation she saw pushed aside any regrets about the haste and secrecy of their wedding.

His eyes skimmed over her slowly, from head to toe and back again. The heat of his gaze was as tangible as a caress, making her skin heat and tingle in anticipation. Desire swept through her, sweeping away the last of her nervousness. Suddenly she was anxious to get through the ceremony and move on to the wedding night—even if it was still the afternoon.

Jason's lips curved, as if he knew exactly what she was thinking, and as if he was thinking the same thing. And she felt a surge of renewed confidence that everything would work out. Because certainly a man who looked at her the way he was looking at her, who wanted her as he had proven he wanted her, had to have real feelings for her. And that gave her hope that, in time, he might grow to love her as she loved him.

Jason spoke his vows clearly and confidently. Penny's voice wasn't nearly as clear or confident, but the words came from her heart as much as her lips. And as she recited her lines she silently prayed that this marriage would last, not just until their babies were born, but "so long as we both shall live."

Then the minister pronounced them husband and wife and told Jason that he could kiss his bride, and Penny braced herself for the perfunctory touch of his mouth against hers.

Except there was nothing at all perfunctory about his kiss.

His lips came down on hers, soft but firm, possessive and persuasive. She had no intention of revealing the feelings she'd only just acknowledged to herself. But the stirring in her blood was all too real, and despite her intentions, her eyelids drifted shut, her arms went around him and she kissed him back.

Chapter Ten

After the ceremony was concluded, Penny and Jason were ushered to a private dining room with a single table set with pristine white linens and sparkling crystal and gleaming silver. There was soft music piped into the room from unseen speakers, audible enough to add to the romanticism of the scene, but not so loud as to interfere with conversation.

The candle inside the hurricane lantern at the center of the table had been lit and there was a tuxedo-clad waiter at the ready with a bottle of nonalcoholic Champagne. He introduced himself as Gabriel, then presented the label for their approval, before popping the cork and pouring the golden liquid into two tall flutes.

In the background, the photographer who had taken pictures during the ceremony continued to snap away, making Penny feel self-conscious about everything she did and said.

Gabriel recited the dinner specials, took their orders, then excused himself to check on the meal preparations in the kitchen.

"Have I mentioned how spectacular you look tonight?" Jason asked, when the waiter had gone.

"Yes, you did," she said, and tried not to remember how her body had heated in response to the obvious appreciation in his eyes when she'd stepped out of the sumptuous dressing room in their suite.

It had been something of a last-minute decision to buy a new dress for the occasion, but in the end she'd decided that a woman's wedding—regardless of the circumstances behind it—warranted a shopping trip. The simple, ivory-colored sheath she'd found was elegant without being fussy, and seemed well-suited to the occasion.

And part of the wedding package Jason had booked was a bouquet for the bride. Hers was a bunch of creamy roses tied with a wide satin ribbon that happened to match the wide ribbon trim on the square neckline and knee-length hem of her dress.

But it was the jewelry she wore that had seemed to catch Jason's eye, for probably the same reason she had hesitated to put it on. Both the earrings that dangled from her lobes and the pendant that sat at the base of her throat held canary diamonds.

For the past six months, Blake had been buying up all of the canary diamonds he could find, trusting that their popularity, and thus their value, would soar when the Santa Magdalena Diamond was found. It had been a gamble, but one that had already started to pay off.

And while Blake brought home the diamonds, Penny was entrusted with the task of designing a series of pieces to spotlight the gems. The resulting collection, traditional Spanish designs reflecting the history of the Santa Magdalena, had recently been spotted on the cover of *Vogue* and on the red carpet in Hollywood.

The earrings she wore—elongated gold filigrees with tiny canary diamonds sprinkled along the bottom like fairy dust—had been a thank-you gift from her brother for the extra hours she'd put in on the project. The necklace—a solid rope-style chain, on which sat a similarly styled pendant—she'd bought for herself, simply because she'd been unable to resist.

Of course, she couldn't have known when she'd chosen her jewelry for this occasion that Jason had also chosen a canary diamond for her, and she couldn't help but wonder if that was just a coincidence…or fate.

"Well, I'll say it again." Jason's words drew her attention back to the moment, as he lifted his glass. "And offer a toast to my beautiful bride."

He, of course looked fabulous in a charcoal-colored suit, pewter shirt and burgundy tie. She'd always thought he looked as if he'd walked off of the cover of *GQ* magazine, but she didn't think she needed to tell him as much. Instead, she said, "And to the quintessential groom," and tapped her glass to his.

The photographer moved a little closer, recording the clinking of crystal and the sipping of wine.

"Is he going to hover around all night?"

Jason shook his head. "Pictures of the wedding night were an additional fee, and while I didn't object to the cost, I wasn't sure you wanted that kind of photographic record."

"I appreciate your discretion," she said, knowing he was only teasing.

But his words also made her think about something she'd been trying not to think about since she agreed to this marriage—the wedding night and every night thereafter. They hadn't really talked about what they each wanted or expected from this marriage, whether it was to be a union in name only or a real husband-and-wife-sleeping-together-in-one-bed relationship. And how the heck was she supposed to ask that kind of question now?

"I think, once he has pictures of us dancing and cutting the cake, he'll leave us alone," Jason said now.

"Dancing and cutting the cake?"

"It's all part of the Ultimate Wedding Package."

"It's been pretty impressive," she admitted. But while she'd been pleased with the details, her attention had mostly been focused on the groom.

"I wanted you to be able to look back on our wedding day and have memories of something better than a ceremony performed by a second-rate Elvis impersonator."

"I'd say you definitely succeeded."

"Then you're not sorry you agreed to this?"

She circled the base of her wineglass with a fingernail as she considered her response. "I think it's too early to tell."

"Not quite the answer I was hoping for," Jason admitted.

She sighed. "We both know that you never would

have proposed—and I would never have considered accepting—if I wasn't pregnant."

"Are you forgetting how you got pregnant?"

"I do remember my sex ed classes," she said, keeping her tone light and trying not to focus on any specific memories of making love with Jason.

"I wasn't actually talking about the logistics, but the attraction that was there from the beginning, the desire that was undeniable, the intensity of the connection between us." His voice was low and seductive. "We were good together, Penny. You know we were."

She lifted a shoulder. "How would I know? I had nothing to compare it to."

"Then you'll have to defer to my knowledge and experience," he said, as he drew her out of her seat and into his arms.

In the low-heeled pumps she wore, she was almost at eye level with Jason. While they'd been dating, she'd appreciated that one of the advantages of going out with a man who was more than six feet tall was that she could wear heels and not tower over him. But not only did she not tower over him, he had a way of making her feel distinctly feminine and completely cherished when she was in his arms.

"In fact," Jason continued, "we were *very* good together."

"What are you doing?"

"We're dancing," he said. "It's a tradition at a lot of weddings."

Yes, at traditional weddings. But this one was anything but traditional. It was certainly nothing like the wedding she'd dreamed of when she was a little girl.

And though it was definitely more than she'd expected, she wasn't going to forget and forgive everything else just because he'd gone out of his way to make the day special.

"I remember dancing with you at Missy Harcourt's wedding," she said now, to remind herself as much as him of his reasons for pursuing her and how all of this had begun.

But Jason wasn't the least deterred by her observation. "That was the first night I held you in my arms. The night I realized I wanted a lot more from you than I was supposed to."

As she swayed in his embrace and listened to his voice skim over her, as sensual as a caress, she knew—despite all of her efforts to the contrary—she was falling under his spell all over again.

"So, if you think this—you and me, here and now—isn't what I wanted, you're wrong," he told her. "It might not be how I planned for things to happen, but I'm not disappointed, and I believe we can make our marriage work."

"This is Vegas, Jason. Where fortunes are won and lost on the flip of a card or the role of the dice. Our marriage vows are as much a gamble as what's happening at all those tables downstairs, and the odds are stacked against us."

His hand skimmed up her back, and even through the fabric of her dress, she felt the heat of his touch—and then the answering fire in her blood.

"I used to think you were a dreamer, not a defeatist." The words were little more than a whisper, as his lips cruised close to her ear.

"I'm a realist," she told him, desperately trying to remember what was real and what was nothing more than a temptingly seductive illusion.

"If you were a realist, you wouldn't be so intent on denying the attraction between us."

"You want to hear that I still want you? Okay—I still want you," she admitted. "I don't want to want you. But apparently my body and my mind are in disagreement on the matter.

"But I also know that having sex with you isn't going to change anything between us. Sure, it might make me feel good for a while, but it won't actually change anything. It certainly won't make me forget that you lied to me or that you dated and slept with me only because you wanted information about Paige's search for the Santa Magdalena Diamond."

"Are you ever going to get over that?"

"Probably not."

"Then you should know that I'm not a martyr."

"Meaning?"

"If all I wanted was information, I would have taken you out a few times and been done with it. I took you to my bed because you were fun and smart and sexy." He drew her closer, forcing her to tip her head back to maintain eye contact. "And because you turned me on like no other woman has in a very long time."

He dipped his head toward her, and Penny knew he was going to kiss her again.

As his mouth inched ever closer to hers, her throat went as dry as the Nevada desert.

Then his cell phone rang.

Jason froze…then swore under his breath when the ring sounded again.

Penny moistened her lips with her tongue, not certain whether she was grateful or annoyed by the interruption. "Don't you think you should answer that?"

"I don't want to answer that," he admitted. "But I left some loose ends hanging at the office, and—"

Another phone began to ring.

She frowned, realizing it was her own.

Jason dropped his arms from around her to reach for his cell, while Penny moved back to the table to get her purse and the phone that was inside.

CALL FROM PAIGE was showing on the display, and the uneasiness that had stirred in her belly when her phone started ringing only moments after his solidified into a nasty ball of fear.

She connected the call. "Paige—what's wrong?"

"Where are you?" her sister demanded, almost frantically. "And how did you know something was wrong?"

"I'm with Jason," Penny admitted, skipping over the details of their secret wedding for the moment.

"Well, I guess that's good then," Paige said. "You can come with him."

"Come with him where?"

"Memorial Hospital."

Penny swallowed. "What happened?"

"It's Mom. I'm not sure what happened. Rex was a little sketchy on the details—and frantic—when he called me. Travis and I are on our way now."

Penny had no idea how long it would take them to get a flight back to Dallas, and then to the hospital from the airport, but she responded, "We'll see you there."

* * *

Jason knew how to make things happen, but even with his guidance and connections, it took more than three hours to get from the hotel in Vegas to the hospital in Dallas. By that time, Eleanor had been in and out of surgery and moved from recovery to a private room.

"Appendicitis," Blake explained to Penny and Jason when they finally arrived. "It was a close call, but the doctors managed to remove the organ before it ruptured."

Penny's eyes filled with tears of relief. "Thank God."

Her brother smiled. "Yeah, we've been doing a lot of that."

Jason squeezed her hand, then asked, "Where's my dad?"

"He's with my mom. Charlie's in there, too. They're only letting her have two visitors at a time right now, so we've been taking turns."

"Where are Tate and Tanya?" Penny asked.

"They were here earlier," Blake told her. "They waited until she was out of surgery, but then they had to take off because Tanya has some kind of big project deadline coming up."

"Gabby and Rafe were here, too," Katie said.

"And Zane and Melanie and Olivia," Paige added. "In fact, you were probably coming up in one elevator while they were going down in another."

Which she knew was her sister's somewhat subtle way of prompting Penny to explain why she was so late in arriving.

"I got here as soon as I could. I mean, *we* got here as soon as we could," she said, including Jason in her explanation. "We were out of town. In Las Vegas, actually."

"Las Vegas?" Blake frowned.

"What were you…" Katie's question trailed off, the answer obviously coming to her as her gaze dropped to Penny's left hand and her eyes widened. "Oh."

It wasn't quite how she'd planned to share the news, but she felt guilty for showing up after all the waiting and worrying had been done by her siblings, and she wanted to explain the reason for her delay.

"Penny and I got married," Jason confirmed, for anyone who hadn't jumped to that conclusion as quickly as Katie.

"You always had to be the first at everything," Travis teased his brother. "I got engaged, so you jumped ahead and got married."

"Expediency seemed prudent under the circumstances," Jason replied easily.

"Well, congratulations." Travis hugged his brother, then his new sister-in-law. "And welcome to the family. Again."

"Thanks." Penny hugged him back, then hugged her sister.

"I can't believe you really did it," Paige said. "And without telling me."

Penny wasn't sure how to respond to that, and was grateful that Charlie's arrival shifted the topic of conversation to Eleanor.

"Rex just wanted a few minutes alone with Mom," he said. "But she's awake and lucid and everything's fine."

When Jason excused himself to step outside of the waiting room to keep an eye out for his father, Blake took the opportunity to shift closer to his youngest sister.

"Are you okay?" Blake asked her. "Is this marriage really what you want?"

Penny nodded. "It surprised me to realize it," she admitted. "But, yes, this is what I want."

"Then I'll say congratulations," Blake said, and kissed both of her cheeks. "And good luck."

She smiled. "You could try to sound a little less cynical when you say that."

"I'm sorry. I really do wish you the best. I'm still just a little wary when it comes to the Foleys, I guess."

"I can understand that," she said. "But I really think Jason and I can make this work."

"If he makes you unhappy, you let me know."

She smiled again. "I love you, Blake."

He hugged her tight. "Right back atcha, sis."

When Rex finally made his way down the hall from Eleanor's room, Jason couldn't help but notice that his father—always the epitome of calm—was a wreck. His eyes were shadowed, his face was pale and drawn, and his hair was in disarray, as if he'd been repeatedly running his hands through it.

Jason could understand why his father had been so worried. He had known a guy in college who had an emergency appendectomy to remove the inflamed organ before it could rupture, so he knew how dangerous a ruptured appendix could be. Thankfully, Eleanor's surgery had been successful, but that didn't help Jason know what to say to his father.

In fact, he felt as helpless now as he did when his mother had died. Of course, Jason had been ten when Olivia Marie passed away, and Eleanor wasn't going to die; but clearly Rex had worried that she might, that he might lose her as he'd lost his first wife.

He saw the lingering fear in his father's eyes, and it was, in his opinion, just one more reason not to fall in love, one more reason not to give away his heart completely, as he'd given it to his college girlfriend, Kara, so many years before. Because he knew that if he did, he would be left with nothing when the woman he gave it to was gone. He'd learned that lesson when Kara died while there was still so much unresolved between them. The tragic end of her young life had left him feeling guilty and confused and unhappy. And that was something Jason wasn't ever going to risk again.

Penny and Paige slipped out of the waiting room to steal a quick moment with their mother, so Jason asked his dad if he wanted to go down to the cafeteria to grab a cup of coffee. But Rex declined the invitation, not wanting to be too far away from his wife.

It was only about ten minutes later that Penny and Paige came back.

"Mom kicked us out," Penny said.

"Apparently, she didn't need all of her kids to come running over something as insignificant as appendicitis," Paige added.

"Insignificant?" Rex was on his feet again, too agitated and worried to sit. "Her appendix nearly ruptured inside of her. She could have died."

The raw anguish in his voice left no one in any doubt about the depth of his feelings for the woman he'd married.

Jason wondered what it would be like to love so deeply, to risk so much, and thanked his lucky stars that his union with Penny was based on practical considerations, and that neither of them wanted or expected a relationship characterized by that kind of all-consuming emotion.

Instinctively Penny reached out, touching Rex's arm, reassuring him. "But she didn't. Because you got her here in time."

"Yeah," he agreed, though he didn't sound mollified. "But it was too damned close for comfort."

Paige kissed his cheek. "Well, thanks. For being there for her. For everything."

"I wouldn't be anywhere else," he assured them.

Jason knew it was true. His father had always been devoted to his family. And now his family included Eleanor, and Eleanor's children were part of the family, as well—including the new daughter-in-law he didn't yet know was his daughter-in-law, because he'd been with his new wife when Penny made the announcement to the rest of the family.

"Mom was asking for you," Penny told Rex.

"Is it okay?" His gaze moved from Eleanor's daughters to her eldest son. "Do you mind?"

"Go ahead," Blake said. "You're the one she wants right now."

There was no bitterness in the words, and Jason knew there could have been, as the rekindling of Rex's romance with Eleanor would have inevitably reminded Blake that his mother had only married Devon McCord because she was pregnant with him.

"Thanks," Rex said, already on his way back to his wife's room.

Jason wasn't clear on all of the details of those past relationships, but he knew enough to be grateful that neither he nor Penny had been involved with anyone else immediately prior to hooking up. If their relationship didn't work out, they would have no one to blame but themselves.

Maybe Penny was right—maybe the odds were stacked against them. But Jason never backed down from a challenge, and he never saw failure as an option.

Penny held back a smile as she watched her new stepfather practically race down the hall to his wife's side. She'd had some reservations when she realized her mother and Rex had married so hastily, but after her conversation with Eleanor in the library—was it really only eight days ago?—she accepted that her mother was truly happy with her new husband, probably happier than she'd ever been before. And while she was happy for her mother, she was also a little envious because she didn't know if she would ever love anyone the way her mother loved Rex, or if she would ever be loved the same way.

Jason had married her, but she had no illusions about his feelings for her. All she had were hopes and dreams. Hope that he would someday grow to love her as much as she loved him, and the dream that they would live happily together as a family.

"She's going to be okay." Jason, obviously misinterpreting the reason for her silence, slid an arm across her shoulders.

Penny nodded. "I know. I just didn't expect that it would shake me up this much. I mean, it was just appendicitis, but maybe it's because it came so close on the heels of her breast cancer scare that I'm being forced to accept that she won't be here forever."

"But you're not going to lose her anytime soon," he said.

"No, thank God." And then she remembered, and she winced. "I'm sorry."

"For what?"

"For being insensitive. I didn't even think about the fact that you've already lost your mom."

"A long time ago."

"I don't imagine that makes it any easier."

Jason shrugged, not wanting to think back, to admit how big a hole had been left in his life when his mother was gone. It had been his first real experience with death and with grief.

Yeah, he'd only been a kid when his mom died, and he'd been devastated. But he'd been wise enough to see the effect that her death had on his father, to realize that the day they buried his mother he'd lost a part of Rex, too. And he realized that loving someone meant giving them a piece of your heart, and that once that piece had been given, you could never get it back. He'd vowed then that he would always protect himself from loving and losing so much.

A valiant objective for a ten-year-old boy, but as the years passed and his grief faded, so did his resolve. He started dating in high school, had some minor flirtations and more serious crushes, but he still didn't know what it meant to really love someone. Then he met Kara Richardson in college.

Loving—and losing—Kara had renewed his determination. Since her tragic death, he never let anyone else get too close, never let himself fall in love again.

Not that he'd ever been tempted, really. At least not until Penny.

Now—well, it was a little late to be having second thoughts about making Penny his wife, and soon she would be the mother of his children. It was almost too easy to imagine a future with her, living side-by-side with her, raising their children together, growing old together, maybe even loving one another.

No, he wasn't going to go down that road again.

No way.

His brother nudged him with an elbow, forcing his thoughts back to the present.

"I think it's time to take your wife home," Travis said, nodding toward Penny.

She was nestled in a vinyl chair by the door and struggling to keep her eyes open. He knew she tired easily these days because of the pregnancy, and today had been a long and emotionally draining day for her, something he should have realized without his brother pointing it out to him.

He went to her and took her hand to draw her out of the chair. She came without protest, a testament to how truly exhausted she was.

"We'll check back in tomorrow," Jason announced to her family. "But for now, I'm taking Penny home."

Except that after they'd said their goodbyes and left the hospital, one important question remained unanswered: where was home?

Penny woke up when the car stopped moving and the engine shut off. It took her a moment after that to realize she was in Jason's car and that his car was parked in her mother's driveway.

As he'd already climbed out of the driver's seat and was coming around to open her door. She had to wait until he'd done so before she could ask "What are we doing here?"

He shrugged. "I just thought, with everything that's happened today, you might feel more comfortable staying here tonight."

"Oh. Yeah. Thanks." She wasn't sure if she sounded grateful or disappointed or just tired. Because she wasn't sure if she was grateful or disappointed, but there was no doubt about the tired.

"We never talked about where we were going to live," Jason said, as he walked with her up to the door.

"We never talked about a lot of things."

"I'd like you to move into my place."

She was tempted to argue, maybe because she'd gotten so used to arguing about everything, but when she thought about it, she realized it made sense. She was going to have a baby of her own, she needed a home of her own; she couldn't expect to continue living at her parents', especially now that she was married. And now that Eleanor had married Rex.

Besides, Jason's downtown condo, though not as big or fancy as his penthouse in Houston, had a spare bedroom that could be converted into a nursery, and it was conveniently located near Foley Industries' Dallas office and McCords' flagship store.

But even while they'd been dating, when she asked why he didn't come to Dallas more, so they could spend more time together, he'd insisted that his base of operations was in Houston. More importantly, Barb, his secretary-slash-assistant, was in Houston, and he couldn't manage without her.

Of course, that might have been just his excuse to keep things from getting too serious between them, because while she'd had illusions of a relationship, he'd only been on a fact-finding mission. Now that they were married, he must have reconsidered.

"You're going to move to Dallas?" she asked, seeking clarification on that point.

Jason frowned. "No. I was referring to my place in Houston."

Her heart sank. "I can't move to Houston."

"Well, you can't expect that I would move to Dallas."

"Why not?"

"Because my office is in Houston."

"You have an office in Dallas, too," she reminded him.

"My base of operations is Houston."

"Mine is Dallas."

He let out a long-suffering sigh. "It's been a long day, Penny, do you think maybe we could argue about this tomorrow?"

"I don't want to argue about this at all."

"Could have fooled me," he muttered.

She narrowed her gaze. "If you think you can just issue orders and I'm going to blindly obey, think again. I'm your wife, not your puppet."

"I don't want a puppet," Jason assured her. "What I want is to have a rational conversation."

"Are you suggesting that I'm being irrational?"

"I'm suggesting that we should table this discussion until we've both had some sleep."

"Fine," she said, because to argue such a logical point might be construed as irrational.

"Thank you." He leaned over to brush his lips against her cheek. "Good night, Penny."

The man she'd married only a few hours earlier, who had given every indication of being interested in a real wedding night while they were in Vegas, had just walked away after kissing her cheek.

Her *cheek*.

"Good night," she replied, more baffled now than tired.

But he was already gone.

Chapter Eleven

Jason picked her up in the morning to take her back to the hospital. Penny claimed that she didn't need him to drive her, reminding him that she had both a license and a car of her own, but he felt strongly that—less than twenty-four hours after they'd exchanged wedding vows—they should at least give the appearance of a united couple. Throughout the drive, though he was sure they were both thinking about their unfinished discussion from the night before, neither of them mentioned it.

He popped into Eleanor's room to say hi to his new mother-in-law, who congratulated him enthusiastically on having the good sense to marry her daughter; then he claimed that he had some things to do at the office, promising to come back to get Penny in a couple of hours.

There wasn't anything urgent going on at Foley Industries. After all, it was Saturday, and he'd expected to still be in Vegas with his bride. Obviously, his father's call had come at the right time, because if they hadn't been interrupted, he would have made love with Penny. And although he knew he would have enjoyed every minute of it, in the bright light of day—without her subtle scent fogging his brain—he realized that intimacy between them might not be the best way to keep their emotions out of the mix.

When he returned to the hospital later, it was with a renewed determination to keep their relationship within clearly established boundaries.

As they were leaving the hospital, Penny said, "Paige invited us to meet her and Travis for dinner tonight."

"I'm not feeling very sociable," he told her.

"I suggested we have dinner at your condo instead of meeting at a restaurant somewhere."

"Well, call her and tell her that something came up."

"What something?" she demanded.

"I don't care what you tell her, but I'm not in the mood for another interrogation by your sister."

"Who is now your sister-in-law," she pointed out. "And who is also engaged to your brother."

"Fine," he said, though it was anything but. "We'll have Travis and Paige over for dinner."

"*I* intended to anyway," she told him.

He scowled. "You would really have gone ahead with your plans without me?"

"I'm not going to fall in line with whatever you want whenever you want, like—" she snapped her jaw shut, leaving the rest of the statement unfinished.

"Like what?" he asked. "Or should I say—like whom?"

"Dinner's at six."

Clearly, she wasn't going to answer his question. Of course, he didn't need to be a rocket scientist to figure it out. She only had one sister, and Paige wasn't the type to be told anything by anyone. Which meant that Penny had to be talking about her mother.

Eleanor didn't strike Jason as a doormat, either, and he knew his father would never have fallen for a woman who didn't have her own ideas and opinion. But he'd heard stories about Devon McCord ruling everything in his domain—business and family included—with an iron fist. Not that he actually used his fists, at least as far as Jason knew, but there were a lot of ways to manipulate and control, and he sensed that Penny had witnessed enough to vow that she wouldn't let herself be subjected to the same.

In fact, two of the things he'd most admired about Penny while they were dating were the sharpness of her mind and the strength of her convictions. Maybe not as much as he'd admired her sexy body, but any man who claimed to be more attracted to a woman's mind than her body was either a liar or not getting any.

He sighed and resigned himself to admiring her mind, because he didn't think he was going to be in a position to admire anything else, anytime in the near future.

Jason grilled steaks for dinner, which he served with baked potatoes, green salad and warm, crusty rolls. Conversation flowed easily around the table, and Penny gradually relaxed, accepting that it was unlikely her sister and her husband would come to blows. In fact, they weren't just civil to one another but almost friendly.

When Paige went to the kitchen to dish up the

cheesecake she brought for dessert, Penny automatically followed to help her.

"You're worried about something," she noted, as her sister carefully lifted the chocolate-caramel-pecan confection out of the box.

"Nope, just thinking about how much I've been dying to taste this."

"Come on, Paige. I know you better than that."

Paige took the knife her sister handed her. "Okay, I guess I was thinking—and maybe worrying a little—about the fact that you're actually married."

"You said I should get married."

Paige sliced through the cake. "I said you should *think* about it."

"I did think about it," Penny said. "And then I did it."

"What changed your mind?"

"It wasn't any one thing, really." She resisted the urge to tell her sister it had been two things, because she and Jason had decided they would keep the news of the twins to themselves, at least for a while. "I guess I just finally decided that if he was so determined to be there for me and our baby, I would let him."

"I think there's more to it than that," Paige said.

Penny handed her a stack of plates. "What else could it be?"

"I think you're still in love with him."

Her sister always had had a sixth sense when it came to knowing what was on Penny's mind—and in her heart. "I don't know what my feelings are right now," she said, unwilling to admit to anyone else the feelings she'd just recently acknowledged to herself.

"Are you happy?" Paige asked gently.

Penny sighed. "I don't know if it's the pregnancy hormones or our history or my own insecurities, but one minute I'm excited and optimistic, confident that we can make this work. The next I feel this overwhelming sense of disappointment and doom, as if I've just made the biggest mistake of my life." She added forks to the plates. "He wants me to move in with him."

"Your husband?" Paige feigned shock. "What is he thinking?"

Penny smiled. "Okay, I know I sound ridiculous, but it's just another one of those things we never talked about before we got married."

"Well, you'll have lots of time to talk now."

"His penthouse is in Houston. I work in Dallas."

"It's the age of technology—you can work anywhere you want, without being tied to a specific office," her sister reminded her.

"But my doctor's in Dallas, too."

"So you'll come back for your appointments or you'll find a doctor in Houston," Paige pointed out reasonably.

"You're right," Penny admitted. "I guess I'm worried that this is one more thing that Jason is getting his way about."

"It's not a contest."

"I know," she said again.

"And Jason's not Dad," Paige said gently.

"I know that, too. I mean, when I'm thinking logically and rationally, I know. And then I have moments of panic, when I think I've given up my identity to be his wife. And then I have moments of doubt and self-pity, when I'm sure this marriage will never last and then I won't be his wife anymore."

"Honey, you are seriously messed up."

Penny managed to laugh through her tears.

"So, when are you moving?"

"I have no idea."

"Well, if you need any help, let me know."

"A lot of help you'll be, since you're mostly living at Travis's ranch now."

"Can you blame me for not wanting to spend a minute apart from the man I love?"

No, Penny couldn't blame her. She could only hope that someday the man she loved would love her even half as much as Travis obviously loved her sister.

After dessert, Penny decided that Jason should help Paige with the dishes, because she needed to talk to Travis.

"What happened to the one who cooks being exempt from cleanup?" Jason grumbled.

"You grilled steaks, you didn't make coq au vin," Penny said. "Though I'm sure you could, if you wanted to."

Her husband didn't look appeased as he carried the dessert dishes into the kitchen.

Paige picked up the wineglasses. "And since I'm guessing they want to talk about my engagement ring, I'm more than happy to let your wife sneak off with my fiancé for a few minutes." Then she turned from Jason to Penny and warned her sister, "But only a few."

"I'll bring him right back," she promised, nudging Travis toward the French doors that opened onto the patio.

"You've finished the design?" he asked, as soon as she closed the doors, so as not to be overheard by those still inside.

"Last week," she told him. "And I know I should have

sent you the sketch, but—" she pulled the ring out of her pocket and handed it to him "—I thought I'd let you see it in 3-D instead.

"I don't always have a specific customer or inspiration for my designs," she told him. "But I wanted this one to mean something to both of you, something more than just a means of showing off the new gem you discovered together."

"There are a lot of stones," he noted, turning the platinum band to examine it from every angle.

She nodded. "The big one at the center represents the Santa Magdalena Diamond, because it was the search for that which brought the two of you together. The slightly smaller ones on either side represent you and Paige, and the even smaller stones, graduated in size until they're almost just jewel chips at the back of the band, are for all of the little treasures that your future together will bring."

Travis was silent, still studying the ring.

Penny was unaccustomedly nervous as she waited for his verdict. She'd created designs for rich and famous customers around the globe, but no project had mattered to her as much as this one, the ring that would be given to her sister by the man she loved and worn by her forever.

"I know you asked for a design, not a finished product, but I was really excited to see what it would look like, and Edmond had the time to put it together, but—"

"No buts," he finally interrupted to say. "I think it's absolutely perfect."

She exhaled. "Really?"

"Really. And I'm so glad I asked you to do this."

Her personal relief gave way to professional indignation. "You had doubts that I was up to the challenge?"

He shook his head. "But I did wonder if I should have put you on the spot with my request. Because I realized after the fact, that it was a little insensitive to ask you to design an engagement ring for your sister, in light of everything that was going on between you and my brother.

"And for what it's worth," he continued, "I'm really glad things have worked out between you and Jason."

"I wouldn't say they're worked out, but we're working on them."

Travis nodded. "Fair enough."

"Now we should get back inside, so that you can take your fiancée somewhere more private to make your engagement official."

"And so you can be alone with your husband?"

She ducked back into the condo rather than attempt to find an answer to his teasing question.

While Penny and Travis were out on the balcony, Jason was trapped in the close confines of the kitchen with his new sister-in-law. Paige didn't seem nearly as uncomfortable as he felt, but maybe that was because she hadn't seduced his virginal sister. She had, however, been caught sneaking around his brother's ranch—a somewhat lesser violation, perhaps, but a violation nonetheless.

Still, she was the first to break the silence.

"I think I'd like to try your coq au vin sometime," Paige said, offering the proverbial olive branch.

"Because you enjoyed your meal so much, or because getting together for dinner again will give you an opportunity to keep an eye on your sister?"

"You're perceptive," she noted. "And maybe I'm feeling a little guilty, too."

"About ratting me out to your sister?"

"Hardly." She put the salad dressings back in the refrigerator. "About telling her she should marry you."

He smiled at that. "You think you talked her into it?"

"Maybe."

"Penny doesn't do anything she doesn't want to do," he reminded her sister. "Ever. She may look sweet and docile, but she has a spine of steel and a mind to match."

"Hmm." Paige considered him as she wrapped up the leftover cake. "You might understand her better than I gave you credit for."

"I didn't think you'd given me any credit."

"I'm trying," she said. "But that doesn't mean I'm willing to wipe the slate clean."

"I wouldn't dare hope that you would."

"You hurt her, Jason."

He didn't reply to that, because he knew that no glib response could refute the truth of her statement any more than it could reflect how truly regretful he felt.

"She may have a sharp mind and a strong will," Paige said. "But she also has a soft and generous heart, and you took advantage of that."

He finished loading the cutlery and closed the dishwasher door. "I know."

Her brows lifted. "You're not going to offer any explanations or excuses?"

"Not to you."

Paige seemed taken aback by his response at first, but then she nodded. "Take care of my sister."

"I will," Jason promised, then smiled. "If she'll let me."

* * *

After Travis and Paige had gone, Penny felt awkward and uncomfortable being alone with Jason. She'd watched her sister and his brother throughout the evening, and had envied the casual intimacies of two people who were obviously connected on so many levels.

It was ironic, really, because Paige hadn't been with Travis even half as long as Penny had dated Jason, but they were so at ease with one another, so obviously in love.

Penny, on the other hand, was pregnant and married to the father of her babies, but love had never been part of the package.

She felt a pang of longing deep in her heart, and the empty feeling wasn't at all assuaged by Jason's next words.

"I want to head back to Houston tomorrow," he told her.

"You've been away from the office a lot recently," she acknowledged.

He nodded. "But if you need to stay until your mom comes home from the hospital, or—"

"I don't need to stay," she interrupted. "She has Rex, and I'd probably just end up feeling like I was in the way."

"You want to come with me?"

He sounded not just surprised but wary, and she wondered if, despite his invitation the night before, he didn't want her with him in Houston.

"It will be kind of difficult for both of us to be there for our babies, if we're not living together," she said.

"We have some time before the babies come," he reminded her.

"What are you suggesting—that we continue to live apart until after I give birth?"

"No, of course not. I'm just suggesting that, if you need some time, you should take it."

"I don't need time, Jason." She waited a beat. "Do you?"

"No."

His response was both immediate and adamant, and eased the nerves in her tummy a little. The nerves eased a little bit more when he reached for her hand and tugged her down beside him on the couch.

She leaned back, but couldn't quite relax. She didn't have the first clue about being a wife or simply being with the man who was suddenly her husband.

"Did you know that Travis is four years younger than me?" he asked.

She frowned at the question that seemed to come out of the blue. "What does that have to do with anything?"

"He's four years younger than me but two years older than your sister, and you're the same age as Paige, which means that I'm six years older than you."

She'd never thought about the age difference before and she certainly wasn't going to worry about it now. But apparently, he was, so she responded lightly, "That just makes it less likely that you'll throw me away for a younger model in ten years, because I'll still be the younger model."

"There is that," he agreed with a smile.

Then his gaze locked with hers, and his smile slowly faded. His eyes darkened and his head dipped closer. Penny felt her breath catch and her heart pound.

But then he drew back and abruptly pushed himself off of the sofa.

"Come on."

She blinked, confusion and disappointment tangling inside of her. "Where are we going?"

"I'm getting you home so that you can get packed," he said. "It's moving day tomorrow."

Chapter Twelve

Penny awoke early the next morning, filled with both apprehension and excitement. It was, as Jason had called it, moving day. But she knew it was more significant than just moving her clothes from the McCord mansion in Dallas to his penthouse in Houston. It was the day they were finally going to start moving forward with their life together.

Rex brought Eleanor home from the hospital just before lunch, allowing Jason and Penny to share a quick visit with their respective parents before heading out. Penny was pleased to see that her mother was doing so well. In fact, she didn't just look good, she looked radiant, though Penny suspected that had more to do with the care of her husband than the doctors at the hospital.

But after a quick lunch, they said their goodbyes and

headed out. Because she wanted to have access to her own vehicle in Houston, Penny drove her car and Jason drove his. And she realized that four hours alone on the road was a lot of time to think.

Mostly, she thought about Jason and their marriage. She wanted them to get settled and feel comfortable with one another before the babies came along and created further chaos in their lives, but she suspected that wouldn't happen easily. Even though he'd been the one to suggest getting married, she wondered if he felt trapped by the circumstances that had triggered his proposal. But then she remembered the look on his face when he'd seen their babies on the sonogram, and she discarded that thought.

Her mind was still filled with unanswered questions when she followed his car into the parking garage. Or maybe it was the not knowing what Jason wanted from their marriage that had her feeling as nervous as a virginal bride. Ironic, considering that she'd lost her virginity months earlier and her status as a bride two days previously.

Technically, she and Jason were newlyweds, but she didn't feel like a newlywed. In fact, she didn't feel wed at all because, aside from the ring on her finger, absolutely nothing had changed in their relationship since they'd spoken their vows.

In all fairness, they'd been both busy and preoccupied since their quick trip to and from Las Vegas. Now that they were alone together, she was sure that things would change.

Wouldn't they?

* * *

When Lucas, the doorman she remembered from previous visits to the penthouse, came in with her luggage, Jason was on the phone in the den.

"Where would you like your bags, Miss?"

"In the spare bedroom, please, Lucas."

He smiled, pleased that she remembered his name, and went to do her bidding.

He didn't know, obviously, that she and Jason were married, and since she wasn't feeling very married, she didn't bother informing him of the fact. Or maybe she didn't tell him because she didn't want him to wonder why Mr. Foley's wife wouldn't be moving into his bedroom.

By the time he came back to the foyer after delivering her bags, Jason had finished his call.

"Thank you, Lucas," he said, and slipped a no doubt very generous tip into the man's hand.

"Thank *you,* Mr. Foley," Lucas replied, then nodded to Penny and walked out, leaving Jason and Penny alone with a whole lot of tension.

She felt awkward and tongue-tied, like a woman on a blind date, certainly not like a woman who was finally alone with the man she'd married two days earlier.

"Are you hungry?" Jason asked, breaking the silence.

"I'm always hungry these days."

"I've got some pasta sauce in the freezer."

"Sounds good to me."

"I'll put the water on to boil, if you want to unpack."

"Sure," she agreed.

They escaped the awkwardness of the moment by moving in different directions—Jason into the kitchen and Penny down the hall.

She looked around the room she'd claimed as her

own, at least temporarily, and decided it was more than suitable. The dark mission-style furniture contrasted with the natural bamboo flooring and combined with the copper and bronze colors in the bedding and drapes to provide an overall effect that was both attractive and warm. It could use a few feminine touches, perhaps, but Penny hoped she wouldn't be sleeping there long enough for it to matter.

But for now, she unzipped her duffel and began transferring her clothes from the bag to the dresser.

She was nearly finished the task when she heard footsteps in the hall. Glancing up, she saw Jason in the doorway.

His brow furrowed when he realized what she was doing. "Did you forget where the master bedroom was?"

"No," she said. "I just thought we might both need some space. For a while."

His frown deepened. "I thought we'd make this room into a nursery."

She noticed that he didn't actually say he wanted her to share his room and his bed, only that he had other plans for this one.

"We've got almost six months before the babies are due," she reminded him.

He shrugged. "Yeah, I guess that's true."

It seemed to Penny that he was almost relieved by her decision, a belief that was supported when he made no further protest about the sleeping arrangements but only said, "Dinner's ready."

After they'd eaten, Jason said he wanted to catch up on some e-mails, so Penny claimed exhaustion and went to bed.

She thought it was ironic that her first time in Jason's penthouse as his wife was the first time she would be sleeping in the guest room. Not that she expected to get much sleep. How could she, when there were so many questions swirling through her mind? Most notably— how had things gone so wrong so quickly?

Everything had been good when they were in Las Vegas. Better than good. Jason had obviously made an effort to give her a wedding with all of the trimmings, an effort that reminded her of the wonderful man he was, the man she'd started falling for when he crossed a wide hotel lobby to say hello.

Unfortunately, their celebration had been cut short by her mother's emergency surgery, but she didn't understand how or why that would change anything between her and Jason. Because something had definitely changed.

He hadn't kissed her since their wedding. There had been some casually affectionate gestures—a touch of his hand to her arm, a brush of his lips against her cheek—but nothing more than that.

It was as she'd feared: now that Jason's ring was on her finger, the challenge was gone. He had what he wanted, a marriage to the mother of his children, and he wasn't interested in anything more.

But what about what she wanted? Because a marriage in name only wasn't exactly her dream come true.

The problem was, she didn't have the first clue how to go about getting what she *did* want.

By the end of the week, Penny still didn't have any answers.

It wasn't as if Jason ignored her so much as he always

seemed to have excuses for keeping a careful distance between them. If she was cooking dinner, he was on the phone. If she was watching television in the living room, he had work in the den. If she wanted to go for a walk, he had any one of a dozen excuses that rolled easily off of his tongue.

And though Penny was usually a cheerful person, she found herself falling into a funk. She felt so far away from everything that was familiar, everyone she knew. She missed her sister, her mother, even her overprotective brothers, though everyone seemed to be so busy with their own lives she wasn't sure she'd have seen much of them, even if she was still in Dallas. But she wasn't in Dallas, so it wasn't even an option.

Apparently, her dark mood wasn't something she could or did hide very well, because even Jason commented on it when he found her nibbling on a slice of toast in the kitchen Saturday morning.

"Are you okay?" he asked her, pouring himself a mug of coffee from the pot she'd brewed. "You look a little out of sorts."

She shrugged. "I'm just feeling a little lonely, I guess."

"Ouch."

She managed a smile. "Maybe homesick is more accurate."

"You miss your family," he guessed.

"I know you're my family now, too," she said, "but you're hardly ever here. And when you are, you treat me more like a roommate than your wife."

"Because I don't demand dinner when I walk in the door?"

He was joking, but Penny wasn't amused. She was

trying to adjust to all of the recent changes in her life, and he wasn't helping.

"Because you don't demand anything," she told him. "Because you rarely come home before eight o'clock at night, and even when you do come home, I'm not sure you realize I'm here."

"I'm sorry if you've been feeling neglected," he said. "But we have some big projects going on at work, and—"

"I'm not asking you to change your schedule to accommodate me. I don't need to be entertained, just acknowledged. Until they get my office renovated at the Houston store, I'm working from here. Day in and day out, these walls are the only thing I'm seeing."

"You want a change," he guessed.

Which was both a true and wholly inadequate generalization of what she was feeling, and she wondered if he really didn't get it or if he was deliberately misunderstanding her.

"I want to spend some time with you."

"Okay," he said. "Let's go shopping."

Shopping?

Jason almost couldn't believe it when he heard the word come out of his mouth. But truth be told, anything—even shopping—was preferable to being alone with her in his apartment all day. Sure, he could hide out in his den, but it seemed as if he'd been doing a lot of that, and sooner or later, Penny would figure out that he was deliberately distancing himself from her. What she wouldn't know was that he was doing so because it was the only way he could be sure to resist the temptation of her.

But if he couldn't maintain a safe physical distance between them, he could at least add the buffer of a crowd and a public venue. As explicit and prurient as his fantasies might be, it was highly unlikely he would be overcome by lust in the middle of a shopping center on a Saturday afternoon.

They started at a major home décor center, and he willingly followed her around, looking at window coverings and throw pillows and lamp shades.

"What do you think of that rug?" she asked, pointing to a carpet on display against a wall.

He shrugged, deciding it was inoffensive, if not particularly appealing. "Where would you put it?"

"In the dining room."

"Sure," he agreed.

"You didn't even look at the price."

He shrugged again. "If you want it, the price is irrelevant."

She shook her head. "What I want *isn't* a dining room rug."

"What is it?" he asked, aware that he might not want to hear her answer.

But she only shook her head again. "You had a professional decorate your home. Who am I to change anything?"

"You're my wife," he reminded her. "And it's your home now, too."

She didn't say anything, and he couldn't begin to guess what she was thinking. He always thought she was one of the most open and honest people he'd ever known, but lately he hadn't been able to get a read on her at all. On the other hand, maybe it wasn't Penny who was making the reading difficult but the distance he was deliberately keeping between them.

"And there is one room that definitely needs some work," he prompted her.

"The nursery?" she guessed, and seemed to brighten a little.

And that was how they ended up at Baby World.

If Jason was to make a list of his top-ten favorite things to do on a Saturday, Penny couldn't imagine that shopping would make the cut. That he was happily browsing the aisles of Baby World left her speechless.

It was Jason who pointed out, logically, that they needed to get some things so they would be ready for the babies' arrivals. Although they still had several more months before then, Penny agreed. Besides, she thought it might be fun to shop with him, to pick out cribs and playpens and high chairs, and it was—but Jason wasn't ready to stop there.

He picked up an enormous stuffed dog with big floppy ears and a ridiculous bowtie in place of a collar.

Penny shook her head. "We have to fit two cribs, a change table, and probably a rocking chair in that room. There is no room for that ridiculous dog."

Jason frowned at her disapproval but put the dog back on the shelf.

As they browsed through the clothing aisles, a little sleeper caught Penny's eye. It was white velour with tiny yellow ducklings marching across the front, and it was absolutely the sweetest thing she'd ever seen.

Unable to resist the impulse, she lifted the hanger off the rack and touched a fingertip to one of the fuzzy little tails.

"Is a baby really supposed to fit into that?" Jason asked. "It's tiny."

"Babies are tiny," she told him, and, with a last glance, replaced the hanger on the rack.

"Why did you put it back?" Jason asked her.

"It's too early to be buying outfits," she said, though she couldn't deny that she was tempted. "Besides, we don't know if we're having girls or boys or one of each."

"It's white and yellow," he pointed out, taking not just one but two of the sleepers off the rack again and tossing them into the cart. "Do you want to find out?"

"Find out what?" she asked, her attention on the sleepers he'd added to the rapidly growing pile of items in the cart.

"If the babies are girls or boys or one of each."

"I don't know." She'd been thinking about it, considering the pros and cons, but was still undecided. "Do you?"

"Yeah," he answered without hesitation, obviously having given the matter some thought himself. "I think it would be more fun to plan and prepare. And it would definitely be easier to pick out names."

"Do you have a preference?"

"For names?"

She shook her head. "Gender."

He considered. "I know I'm supposed to say I don't, that so long as the babies are healthy nothing else matters. And that is the most important thing," he agreed. "But if I could choose, I think I'd really like at least one girl."

"You want a girl?"

"Why does that surprise you?"

She shrugged. "I just figured...I mean, most men want boys to continue the line and carry the family name."

"A lot of women keep their family names when they marry. You did."

There was something in his tone—disappointment, maybe—that caught her off guard. "Does that bother you?"

"It shouldn't," he admitted. "But in some ways, it seems as if it's not legal, not real. I'm still Jason Foley and you're still Penny McCord."

"You could change your name."

"Yeah, that would go over big with my family."

She didn't know what to say. She wasn't sure why she hadn't changed her name when they married, unless it was for the reason that he'd guessed—because their marriage didn't feel real.

Or maybe because she hadn't been sure it would last.

She was an optimist by nature, but only a week after their exchange of vows, she was already wondering how long they could go on with the way things were between them—and she was slowly driving herself crazy trying to figure him out.

She knew he was still attracted to her. Maybe if she'd been farther along in her pregnancy, she might have doubted that, but though the changes in her body were obvious to her, she had barely begun to show. And she'd caught that look in his eyes—the heat, the desire, the need—when he thought she didn't see him looking.

For goodness' sake, they were married. She was his wife, soon to be the mother of his children, and all those pregnancy hormones racing through her body—not to mention the effect of his proximity—were combining to drive her insane with wanting.

So why was he holding back? Why was he so determined to maintain this charade of friendship? What was going on with him?

What was going on with him was that Jason had figured out the only way to keep Penny from mattering too much was to compartmentalize their relationship and his feelings for her.

First she'd been his lover, then she'd become his wife, and somewhere in between, they started to be friends. In just a few more months, she would also be the mother of his children. And the more time they spent together, the more the lines between the titles and roles became blurred. But there was still one line that he had not crossed.

And if he crossed that line, if he gave in to the urge to make love to her—and there was no doubt about those urges—there would be no compartments. She would be his wife, his friend, his lover. His everything.

And if he lost her, he would lose everything. Just as he'd lost everything when Kara died.

That was a risk he wouldn't take again.

So he ignored her signals. The way she touched him, or brushed against him, or looked at him. It wasn't easy, but he managed.

He was in the den Tuesday night, not really working so much as avoiding his wife, when she tracked him down. He focused on the e-mail that was open in front of him, without really seeing the words, all too conscious of Penny hovering in the doorway, waiting for him to look up, to acknowledge her.

He'd always thought his penthouse was a little too big, that there was too much space. Since Penny had moved in, he felt as if the walls were closing in on him.

It wasn't really as bad as that, and it wasn't her fault. It's just that he couldn't go anywhere in the whole damn apartment without stumbling across some sign of her presence—a bouquet of fresh flowers in an old milk bottle in the kitchen, a glass vase filled with river rocks in the dining room, some scented leaves and flowers in a bowl in the bathroom. Everywhere he turned, he saw her, smelled her, wanted her.

The only rooms that bore no evidence of her presence were those she hadn't stepped foot into since moving in: the master bedroom and bath. But they weren't devoid of memories. Every night when he crawled into his king-size bed, he pictured her there, naked and rumpled and tangled in the sheets, a sleepy smile curving her lips. And every time he stepped into the shower, he remembered her there—her long, lean limbs slick with the soap he'd rubbed over her body.

He forced the tempting memories aside and glanced up from the computer screen.

"I don't want to disturb you, if you're in the middle of something," she said.

"Nothing that can't wait," he said, unwilling to admit exactly how much she disturbed him—every minute of every day.

"I was just wondering if you knew where our marriage certificate was."

"It's in the filing cabinet. Why?"

"I need a notarized copy to register my change of

name," she told him. "I didn't think too much about it before, or I would have done it automatically when we got married."

"Why are you doing it now?" he asked.

"Because I want to prove to you that I'm committed to this marriage."

Boundaries, he reminded himself.

He might have been a little annoyed, maybe even disappointed, that she'd remained Penny McCord after their exchange of vows. But then he'd realized that the name was a symbolic barrier, a confirmation that their marriage hadn't blurred all of the lines, and he needed that barrier now.

"You don't have to prove anything to me."

"I'm not doing it for you. I'm doing it for us."

That was what he was afraid of—that she was thinking in terms of "us" while he was still trying to keep their lives separate and apart as much as possible.

"Do you have a problem with that?" she asked, when he didn't say anything.

"I'm just concerned that I pushed for too much too soon."

"You're not just talking about the name change," she guessed.

"No, I'm not," he admitted.

"It's a little late to be having second thoughts, isn't it?"

Much too late, he admitted to himself.

But what he said was, "We haven't consummated our marriage."

Penny glanced away, but not before he caught a glimpse of the wounded confusion that clouded her eyes, and he mentally cursed himself. He was doing this so as not to hurt her again, so that neither of them could hurt the other.

"So what happened today?" she finally asked, turning back to him again. "Did you run into an old girlfriend? Or a new prospect?"

"This has nothing to do with anyone else."

"Two weeks ago, you didn't want anything as much as you wanted to marry me and be a father to our babies, and now you want an annulment?"

"I don't want an annulment," he told her, though he wondered if it might have been better for both of them if he did. If he could cut all ties and let her go, to live her life with someone who could give her everything she wanted and deserved in a relationship. Someone whose heart wasn't beyond reach. "But I thought you might."

"I agreed to marry you of my own free will."

"You agreed to marry me because you're pregnant."

She lifted her chin, met his gaze evenly. "And the action that led to that was also of my own free will."

"You were a virgin."

"So? My lack of sexual experience didn't interfere with the working of my brain."

"I took advantage of your inexperience."

She actually laughed at that. "Do you remember our first night together?"

He did, in achingly vivid detail.

"I seduced you," she reminded him.

"You think so?"

"I know I did." Her lips curved in a smile of pure feminine satisfaction. "You didn't even know what hit you."

"Is there a point to this trek down memory lane?"

"I'm getting to it," she assured him, but seemed to go completely off-track with her next question. "Why did you want to marry me, Jason?"

"I thought that was obvious."

"So your decision was based on nothing more than the fact that I'm pregnant?"

"I want to be there for you," he said. "And to be a father to our babies."

"When we got married, when we were dancing at the hotel in Las Vegas, you said that we were good together. You talked about desire and attraction."

"A man will say almost anything to get a woman into his bed."

"And yet, you haven't made any attempt to get me there since that night."

"It didn't seem right to take advantage of the situation."

"You might have talked to me about it," she said, reasonably. "Instead of making me feel as if you didn't want me anymore."

"I didn't want to complicate things."

"And a husband and wife sharing a bed, sharing affection, is a 'complication'?"

"You were the one who wanted to sleep in the guest room," he reminded her.

"Because I didn't want you to assume I'd sleep with you just because we were married."

"Yeah, I got that."

"But it wasn't that I didn't want to sleep with you."

"Huh?"

She huffed out a breath. "Apparently, you didn't get that."

"Penny, it's been a really long day and I don't have

the time or the energy to decipher some complex female code. If there's something you want to say, just say it."

"I love you," she said. "Is that simple and straightforward enough for you?"

He shook his head, battled against the instinctive panic that rose up inside of him upon hearing those words. He didn't want her to love him, and he sure as hell didn't want to love her.

"You don't love me," he said. "You're just romanticizing the situation."

"For goodness' sake, do you think I wanted this to happen? Do you think I wanted to fall in love with a man who obviously doesn't want to love me?"

"Then what do you want?"

"I want a real marriage."

He didn't need her to spell it out any more explicitly. And he wouldn't admit that he wanted the same thing. He wouldn't risk blurring the boundaries he'd so carefully maintained.

"I care about you, Penny. You know that I do. But you want more than I can give you."

"Maybe that's true," she said softly. "But why won't you at least try?"

"I can't."

Even if he'd guessed that she wouldn't accept such a vague answer, he still wouldn't have anticipated her response.

"Tell me about her," she said.

He frowned. "About who?"

"Whoever made you afraid to open up your heart again."

"You have quite an imagination," he said, but he didn't quite meet her gaze when he spoke the words.

"And you built up those walls for a reason."

She moved closer, deliberately invading his personal space, as if to push right up against those walls she mentioned and tear them down. But he was more determined not to let her.

"I'll be a good father to our babies and a faithful husband," he said. "But I can't promise you more than that."

"Faithful?" she challenged, taking another step until she was so close her breasts brushed against his chest. So close that when she tipped her head back, her lips— full and soft and tempting—were only inches from his own. "You'd have to actually be sleeping with me to be faithful to me."

The challenge was in her eyes as much as her words, and if there was a man alive who could deny himself the one thing he wanted more than anything else when it was so blatantly offered, that man was much stronger than Jason.

"Is that what you want? Is that what will make it real for you, Penny? If I take you to bed, will that be enough?"

"I don't know." She met his gaze evenly. "But at least it would be a start."

All the warnings of his brain were drowned out by the much louder and more insistent demands of his thoroughly aroused body. He grabbed her wrist. "Let's go, then."

Chapter Thirteen

Penny knew that Jason was trying to shock her into protesting, and that if she pulled back, he would only be too willing to let her go. But she had no intention of pulling away when he needed her so much. Because she'd finally figured out that he did, that he'd been so intent on pushing her away because he was afraid to hold on, afraid to admit his feelings for her. She still didn't understand what was behind that fear, but now that she recognized it, she was determined to help him overcome it.

Once they were in his bedroom, he turned to face her, his eyes dark and unreadable. "You're sure this is what you want?"

"Positive," she said, giving no hint of the knots in her belly as she calmly began stripping her clothes away.

His eyes followed the movement of her fingers, as

she unfastened the row of buttons that ran down the front of her blouse, and the knots intensified.

What if this wasn't what he wanted?

What if she'd been wrong?

But she'd come too far to back down now. She wouldn't give up on their marriage without a fight.

As the silk top floated to the floor, his eyes dropped to her breasts, covered only by whisper-thin black lace. She hesitated only a fraction of a second before unfastening the clip at the front, and then, even that scrap of lace slipped away. His eyes flared, dark and hot.

The intensity of his gaze, the naked heat in his eyes, had her fingers fumbling as they worked the button at the back of her skirt, then the zipper. She pushed the skirt over her hips, let it pool at her feet.

Gone were the days when she worried that she didn't have a model-perfect body. At fourteen weeks into her pregnancy, gone were any hopes of having a model-perfect body. But Jason had never seemed to mind that she was imperfect. In fact, he'd shown her time and again while they were dating that he loved her body—even if he didn't love her. And since it was one of few weapons she had in her arsenal, she was prepared to use it.

As she stripped away the final scrap of lace, she knew she was baring not just her body but her soul.

"Now the question is…is this what you want?" she asked him.

He swallowed. "If you're asking do I want to have sex with you, I'd have to respond with a very enthusiastic 'Yes!'"

But he was still holding back, refusing to give her what she wanted, what they both needed. It was as if he'd dug in his heels so deep, he didn't know how to take that first step.

So she lowered herself onto the edge of the mattress and prompted him with a smile and a crook of her finger. "Then why don't you bring some of that enthusiasm over here?"

He stripped away his clothes, then came to join her on the wide bed. He curled his hand over her shoulder, and the warmth of his palm against her bare skin sent shivers of excitement dancing through her veins. His gaze dropped to her mouth, and her lips parted, anticipating, wanting.

But he didn't kiss her, and though she was disappointed, she wasn't surprised. Kissing was an intimacy he wouldn't allow himself, not now, when he was so intent on making a point. This wasn't about feeling close and connected. It was about sex—raw and uncensored. He wasn't going to pretty it up with soft words or gentle touches.

But she didn't need it to be anything more than what it was: primitive, elemental, real.

He tangled his hand in her hair, pulling her head back. Then he feasted on her throat, using his lips and tongue and teeth to drive her to distraction. She fell back on the mattress, dragged him with her, arching in response to the fast and impatient stroke of his hands over her quivering flesh.

His teeth scraped over her collarbone, his tongue swirled around one peaked nipple, then the other. Her breath was coming in short, fast bursts now, as she fought to draw air into her lungs while the world spun around her.

She cried out in shocked pleasure as the fierce suckling of her breast sent her tumbling off the edge of the first sharp peak of pleasure. Then finally, his mouth came down on hers, hot and hungry, giving nothing while demanding everything.

She let him take and take, and she gave, freely and openly. She held nothing back and offered up everything that was in her heart.

He drove into her, hard and deep and she cried out again, as fresh waves of pleasure crashed over her. She wrapped herself around him, arms and legs holding on to him through the storm of dizzying pleasure.

And then, unexpectedly, his kiss softened, his hands gentled, his strokes slowed. There was no more taking or giving, but sharing. Two bodies joined together, moving together, loving together. And it felt so right, so good, so perfect.

The physical aspect of their relationship had always been spectacular. True, her experience was limited, but she'd heard enough complaints from other women to know she'd been fortunate in choosing a first lover who was so considerate of her needs, who ensured her pleasure before taking his own.

But this…this was beyond spectacular. It was beyond anything she'd ever imagined.

Penny closed her eyes so that he wouldn't see the tears of joy that filled them. Yes, this was what she'd wanted: to truly join together with him—to make love with the man she loved.

She gasped and shuddered and clung while her body tightened around him, and gloried in the pulsing release of his body into hers.

Penny lay motionless beneath him for a long while,

afraid to move, afraid to burst the fragile bubble of happiness that surrounded her. Making love with Jason had been an experience that transcended all others. And she didn't believe for one minute that he could make love to her the way he'd just made love to her unless he was in love with her, at least a little.

Of course, that didn't mean he was comfortable with his feelings, or willing to admit them, as he proved when he rolled away from her and off of the bed. She blinked back a rush of tears as he picked his clothes up off of the floor and began putting them back on. She didn't know why he was fighting so hard to deny what was between them—or how long she could continue to bang her head against the walls he kept building to keep her out.

"At least that puts your annulment argument to rest," she said, keeping her tone light.

He paused in the buttoning of his shirt to glance over at her. "Is that what this was really about?"

"You know what this was really about."

He didn't say anything as he fastened his belt, then turned to face the mirror to straighten the collar of his shirt.

Apparently, she was going to have to bang her head once more.

"I love you, Jason."

He stood for a moment with his back to her, though she caught his gaze in the mirror, and the anguish in his eyes tore at her heart.

But all he said was, "Damn you."

Then he stormed out of the room.

Penny stared at the empty doorway for a long time, as if she could will him to come back. But a few minutes later, she heard the click of the lock and knew he'd not just left the bedroom and the apartment, he'd left her.

She pulled her knees up and hugged them tight against her chest, where her heart was breaking wide-open.

When Jason left Penny in his bed, he didn't know where he planned to go, he only knew he couldn't stay. He wouldn't let himself be sucked into her fantasy. Because that's what love was—an illusion at best, and usually only a temporary one.

"I love you, Jason."

Well, he hadn't asked her to love him. And he sure as hell hadn't wanted to love her.

And he didn't.

She was his wife, the woman carrying his babies, and he fully intended to make a home with her and live together as a family. But he absolutely was not going to fall in love with her.

Too late.

He ignored the taunting voice in the back of his mind, refused to believe it. Nothing had changed between them. Making love with her didn't change anything. Because he'd fallen in love with her long before he'd made love with her again.

And while falling in love sounded easy, like a leisurely descent through the clouds in a hot-air balloon, the reality, at least for Jason, was different. More like a jump from a plane at fifteen thousand feet without a parachute, the realization of his feelings slamming into him with the force of hitting the ground.

He had no idea how or when it had happened. Obviously sometime between their meeting at the Harcourt-

Ellsworth wedding and their own. But it had taken the physical act of lovemaking for him to realize it. The shared intimacy had broken through all that remained of the barriers around his heart. He simply couldn't continue to hold out against her. She was so soft and warm and giving, and he was helpless to resist her.

But old habits die hard, and he wasn't ready to admit that he could or did need anyone else to make his life complete. After all, he was perfectly happy with his life before Penny came along, and he could be just as happy again without her.

So why was he feeling so miserable? And how was he going to be a father to their babies if he walked out on their marriage before they were even born?

They were questions he didn't know how to answer, or maybe he didn't want to accept the answers. At least not yet.

Until he figured it out, he opted to stay at the office where he had a spare shirt in the closet and a couch almost long enough to stretch out on. He had everything he needed—except the softhearted, green-eyed woman who had somehow stolen his heart.

What he didn't think he had—and certainly hadn't expected—was a secretary who returned at ten o'clock that night and caught him trying to stretch out on the couch in his office.

"Don't you have a bed at home?" Barb asked him.

Jason glared at her. "What are you doing back here?"

"I forgot to water the plants."

"That's not in your job description."

"Neither is dispensing marital advice, but apparently I have to do that, too."

"Thanks, but I don't need any advice."

"If that was true, you wouldn't be sleeping on a couch in your office."

"Okay, what's your advice?" Jason asked, figuring, the sooner she said what she wanted to, the sooner she would be gone.

"Take your sorry ass home."

He frowned. "That's your advice?"

"I never claimed to be Dr. Phil."

"And what makes you think I have anything to be sorry for?"

"You're the one who got kicked out of your home."

"She didn't kick me out." Of course, he hadn't stuck around long enough to give her the chance. Instead, he'd run away like the coward he was.

"Then there's no reason you can't go back," Barb said, logically.

No reason, except that he'd done exactly what he'd promised himself he wouldn't do—he'd fallen in love with the woman he married.

He wasn't a man who was easily fazed. He knew how to keep his cool in the face of a crisis. He'd handled the news of Penny's pregnancy; he'd coped with the surprise that she was carrying twins. Yet the realization that he'd fallen in love had sent him into a complete tailspin.

But Jason knew it wasn't really the loving that scared him—it was the possibility that he could lose Penny as he'd lost Kara so many years before.

He didn't come home that night or the next.

Penny could have called Jason on his cell or at the

office, but she didn't think there was any point. She'd said everything she needed to say, and so had he.

Once again she'd been a fool.

The first night he was gone, she cried. She cried for herself, for Jason, for everything they might have had together. She cried until she was sure there were no tears left inside of her. The next day she wallowed in misery and self-pity until a question began to tug at her mind.

If Jason didn't care about her, if her feelings meant nothing to him, why was he running scared? Because, after two days, she realized that was exactly what he was doing.

Well, she wasn't going to chase after him. She'd given him her heart, she was determined to at least hold on to her pride.

She felt a flutter of something in her tummy, like the brush of butterfly wings. Then it came again, and she sucked in a breath as realization stirred along with the babies inside her. Her hand moved instinctively to her belly, her palm splayed protectively over the tiny lives growing in her womb.

Okay, so there were bigger things at stake than her pride.

But the way she figured it, he had to come home sometime, and she would be there when he did. Beyond that, she didn't really have a plan.

Having Devon McCord as a father taught her that the path of least resistance was unquestioning obedience. As a child, she'd done what she was told to do when she was told to do it. As an adult, she'd had to make a conscious effort to break that pattern.

Jason had never tried to tell her what to do. He'd

never made her feel as if she was incapable of making her own decisions. The only doubts she had came from within herself. Doubts that had been planted by her father's criticisms and were nurtured by her own efforts to avoid conflict.

But this time, she wasn't going to sit back and accept whatever came her way. She was going to take control of her life and her future.

The first step was moving out of the guest room. Because she wasn't a guest—this was her home, too, and it was past time she started acting as if she was living there instead of just visiting.

For the most part, she did like Jason's penthouse the way it was. The room she was least fond of, however, was the master bedroom. The walls were a dark green, the furniture was teak, the bedding and window coverings a deep burgundy. While everything coordinated nicely, it was a little dark for her tastes. And if she was going to be sleeping in there—and she planned on it— she would need to make some changes.

She bought a can of sage-colored paint and painted only one wall—the longest one behind the bed. Of course, she had to call building maintenance to get someone to move the bed for her—she wouldn't attempt to move a king-size bed on her own, even if she wasn't pregnant. Then she added new bedding and window coverings in a light tan color, keeping the burgundy and green throw pillows for color, and hung some sepia-tone prints in oversize frames on the dark walls.

When it was done, she fell into bed, exhausted.

Her last thought before she fell asleep was that she would tackle the nursery tomorrow.

* * *

Jason was staring bleary-eyed at the quarterly report on his computer screen when the phone buzzed, not realizing that he was half-asleep until the noise jolted him awake. Three days had passed since he'd walked out on Penny—and so had three endless, sleepless nights.

He reached for the receiver with one hand and his coffee mug with the other. "Yeah."

"Lindsay Conners is on line two."

"Who?" He lifted the mug to his lips, grimaced when he swallowed a mouthful of cold coffee. He must have been dozing longer than he'd realized for his coffee to have chilled so much.

"She said if you didn't recognize the name to tell you that she's the mother of the baby who spit up on your suit."

The fog around his brain cleared. "Oh. Right. Thanks, Barb."

She disconnected and he picked up line two.

Five minutes later, he was sitting across from Lindsay in the café in the lobby.

She was, he noted with surprise, alone. "No kids today?"

She smiled, looking a lot more relaxed than the last time he'd seen her. "No. They're being taken care of by…a friend."

"Are you here about a job? Because I can contact Margaret in HR and…" His words trailed off as she shook her head.

"No, I'm not looking for a job. I just wanted to stop by and thank you for being so kind to me that day on the plane, and for making me remember that there are still some nice guys in the world."

"You didn't need to come over here for that."

"I did," she insisted. "Because when I finally got home that day, and finally got the kids settled, I started thinking about another nice guy, one I hadn't spoken to in a lot of years. Long story short—I'm moving to Alaska."

He wasn't sure if she'd omitted a lot of information or if his sleep-deprived brain was failing to make a logical connection. "You're moving to Alaska…because I held your baby on the plane?"

She laughed. "Because you made me remember Ethan—the man I should have married. Except that I was twenty years old when he proposed and afraid of everything I would miss out on if I tied myself down at that point in my life. So, instead of taking everything that he offered, I turned away.

"Six years later, when I was a little more mature and experienced, I met Brian. Maybe he wasn't the love of my life, but he was the man I was with at the time I was ready to get married and have a family. By the time I realized I never loved him the way I'd loved Ethan— and that he never loved me, either—we had one baby and another on the way.

"I don't regret the years we had together," she said. "Because despite everything else, I ended up with two wonderful kids. But when Brian left, I went through the whole gamut of emotions. I was stunned, hurt, angry, sad. But mostly I was afraid. Afraid that I would never stop hurting, and never have the courage to open up my heart again.

"And then I called Ethan and we talked. I hadn't seen or heard from him in almost fifteen years, but our conversation wasn't in any way awkward or uncomfortable. We talked again the next night, and the night after that, and finally he said, 'Lindsay, are you going to come to me or do I have to come down to Texas to get you?' And I knew that he would do it, because even after fifteen years, he still loves me. And I still love him.

"So that's why I'm taking my kids and moving to Alaska, which is a heck of a lot scarier than anything I faced when I was twenty," she admitted. "But I've finally realized that not everyone gets second chances, and I'm not going to let this one pass me by."

"Well then, I'll wish you luck," Jason said to her.

Lindsay laughed. "I don't need luck, because this time I've got love on my side."

He pondered that comment long after she'd gone, long after he'd let another cup of coffee grow cold, and he marveled at the courage of a woman who had lost so much and was willing to risk it all again. For love.

He'd been in love before. His feelings for Kara had been real—certainly more real than anything he'd ever experienced to that point in his life—but they weren't nearly as deep or as strong as what he felt for Penny.

And after three days away from her, he realized that he'd been using his grief over Kara's death as a shield against loving Penny—and not very effectively. Maybe loving Penny was a risk, but it wasn't as if he had a choice in the matter. Not telling her how he felt certainly hadn't stopped the feelings from growing.

He went back up to his office, marched past his secretary's desk without saying a word, grabbed his coat and his briefcase and walked back out again.

"It's the middle of the day," Barb said. "Where are you going?"

"Home," he said simply, and felt as if an enormous weight had lifted off of his chest.

She huffed out a breath. "Well, it's about time."

Jason followed the pulsing beat of a Van Halen song toward the spare bedroom, and with every step he took, his heart pounded harder against his ribs. He didn't know if Penny was even speaking to him, but at least she was still here. It wasn't until he opened the door of his penthouse and heard the music that he acknowledged the fear, buried deep inside his heart, that he might already be too late, that she might already be gone.

Instead, she was standing on a stepladder, painting the trim around the window, and he just stood for a moment, watching her. She turned to dip her brush in the can of paint and spotted him there.

The paintbrush slipped out of her hand, bounced off a step on the ladder, then against her thigh, before landing on the ground. Jason crossed the room to pick it up carefully by the handle and set it on the tray.

"Good thing you put down drop cloths," he said.

Penny didn't seem to know what to say. She just stared at him with a mixture of hope and wariness in her beautiful green eyes.

He reached for the rag she'd been using, found a clean corner, and started to rub the streak of butter yellow paint on her leg.

She swallowed. "You'll get, uh, paint on your suit."

"I'm not worried," he said, and continued with the task. Then, "I thought you'd be at the store."

"Is that why you came home in the middle of the day—so you could sneak out again without seeing me?"

"No." He put the rag down, looked up at her. "I wanted to see you. I just thought I'd have to wait until you got home to do so."

She started down the ladder, and he stepped back, out of her way. "I decided to take a couple of days off."

"Why?"

"It occurred to me that I needed to make some changes around here if I wanted to feel like it was my home, too."

"Then…you're staying?"

She lifted her chin, almost defiantly. "I'm staying."

He'd been prepared to plead, to beg, to do whatever he needed to do to keep her in his life. And while he didn't think she'd made her decision to make things easier for him, he was both relieved and grateful. "I'm glad."

"Are you?"

He nodded. "I've missed you."

"No one told you to go," she said, silencing an exuberant David Lee Roth with the press of a button. "Or to stay away."

"I know. I just needed some time." And though she didn't ask, he told her, "I've been sleeping at the office. Or maybe it would be more accurate to say I've been trying to sleep at the office."

"Your choice," she reminded him.

"Yes, it was," he agreed. "And not one of the smartest choices I ever made."

"And now?" she prompted.

"Now I want to come home," he said. "To be with you, to start our life together. But I understand, if that's going to happen, I need to be honest with you about some things. I need to tell you about Kara."

Penny sat on the edge of the bed that was covered by an old sheet to protect it from paint splatter. He sat on the blanket chest so that he was facing her, so close that their knees almost touched.

"We met when I was in my second year of college, she was a drama major—bright and fun and beautiful. And I was completely infatuated.

"It wasn't all smooth sailing," he told Penny. "In fact, it wasn't smooth at all. She started to demand more and more of my time, she was clingy when we were out in public, and when we weren't together, she accused me of being with other girls. Of course, the more possessive she got, the less I wanted to be with her. We broke up. We got back together.

"She seemed to thrive on the constant drama, but it made me crazy. So, at the end of the year, after we both finished our exams and were going our separate ways for the summer, I suggested that we take a break.

"She cried and pleaded, but she'd been crying and pleading for months, and I couldn't deal with it anymore. I came home for the summer and went to work at Foley Industries. With every day that passed, I half-expected she would show up—it was the kind of thing she would do—but she never even called. A few weeks later I learned, through a mutual friend, that she'd got a minor part in a stage production in some little town not far from where she lived.

"I went up one weekend to check out the play, and we had a great couple of days together. She seemed happier, more secure about who she was and what she was doing, and we talked about getting back together when we returned to school in September. She called me a few weeks later to invite me to come up for the year-end cast party. I had responsibilities at my job and couldn't get away, and she got ticked. She accused me of caring more about my job than her, and then she hung up on me.

"I should have called her back, tried to make her understand. Or maybe I should have taken the time off of work because I knew it meant a lot to her. But I didn't—and as it turned out, that was the last conversation we ever had.

"She went to the cast party with her friends, and I don't know if there was alcohol or drugs or both— Kara was always game to try anything at least once— but she ended up falling off of a bridge into the river below and drowning."

"Oh, Jason." There were tears of empathy in Penny's eyes as she reached out to take both of his hands in hers. "I'm so sorry."

"I felt so lost and so guilty. My experience with Kara taught me to be wary, to never let myself get too deeply involved. I didn't want anyone to matter that much again. I certainly had no intention of ever falling in love again." He leaned forward and kissed her. Softly, gently. "You blew all my plans to pieces by making me fall in love with you."

Her breath caught, the fingers that were linked with his gripped tighter. "What did you just say?"

He smiled. "I love you, Penny. Maybe it took me a while to realize it, but I finally did. Kara was my past. You are my present and my future. And I know that there are no guarantees in life, but I want a life with you. For now and forever."

"Well, that works out pretty good," she said. "Because that's what I want, too."

Then she wrapped her arms around him, pressed her mouth to his, and as Jason sank into the kiss, engulfed in the warmth of her embrace, he knew that he was finally home.

Chapter Fourteen

Penny was awakened by a kiss on Christmas morning. She lifted her arms without opening her eyes, winding them around Jason's neck to pull him closer.

"You're going to make me forget that I'm holding a breakfast tray," he warned against her lips.

Her eyes flickered open. "You brought me breakfast in bed?"

"Just some cinnamon rolls I heated up, and some fresh fruit and yogurt."

She shifted into a seated position so that he could set the tray across her lap.

"This is so sweet."

He shrugged. "Well, everyone does the decorating of the tree and hanging of stockings, but I thought we should start some Christmas traditions of our own."

"I like this one," she said, stabbing a plump ripe strawberry with her fork and popping it into her mouth.

"Well, hurry up with it," he said, "because we have to check under the tree to see what Santa brought."

"Santa only delivers presents to good girls and boys," she teased.

"Wasn't I good last night?"

Her lips curved. "Very good," she agreed. "Though I'm not sure the jolly old elf concerns himself with the type of behavior you're referring to."

But she dutifully finished her breakfast, sharing bites and nibbles and kisses with Jason, then got out of bed and slipped her robe on over her nightshirt.

There was a veritable mountain of presents under the huge balsam fir that was propped up in the corner of the living room. Certainly a lot more than had been there when she'd gone to bed the night before. And more than half of them were "from Santa," according to their labels.

When opened, she found a ton of baby things—rattles and bibs, board books and teddy bears, and two impossibly small Texas Rangers baseball jerseys.

"Obviously, Santa enjoyed shopping at Baby World as much as you did," she teased her husband.

Jason just smiled as he tore at the paper on one of his presents.

She'd struggled, trying to pick out gifts for her new husband. But she'd found the complete series of one of his favorite television shows, a luxurious cashmere sweater that matched the blue of his eyes, a new putter he'd coveted when they were shopping together for a gift for his father, and—after much debate—she'd gone back to Baby World and bought the big floppy dog that he'd been so disappointed about having to put back.

For Penny, Jason had the babies' sonogram picture framed and he gave her a coffee-table book about Venice. When she flipped open the cover, a pair of plane tickets fell out.

"Because I want to take you for dinner at the real St. Mark's Square," he told her. "And I figured we better go sooner rather than later, because you won't be able to travel in a few months."

"The time seems to be flying by so fast," she admitted. "I can hardly believe that by this time next year, we'll have two babies crawling around."

"Probably trying to pull down the Christmas tree," Jason warned.

"Ripping bows off of presents," Penny added.

"Wanting to eat the ornaments."

"And generally running both of us ragged."

But she smiled after she said it, and he couldn't help but smile back.

"Are you still scared?" she asked.

He wrapped his arms around her, pulling her close. "Terrified."

She leaned her head back against his shoulder. "Me, too."

"But I figure we can handle anything together."

"I hope— Oh."

Jason turned her around, so that she was facing him. "What is it? What's wrong?"

But Penny only smiled as she took his hand and laid it on the curve of her belly.

"What…it moved. He moved. They moved. One of them moved."

She laughed. "Yeah."

"Have you felt it—him—them—before?"

"A couple of times," she said. "But never as strong as that."

The flutter came again, and Jason's eyes went wide. "Wow."

"It's pretty amazing, isn't it?"

"You're amazing," he told her, pulling her into his arms. "Thank you."

She tipped her head back. "For what?"

"For not giving up on me."

"I love you," she said simply.

"Well, that's good," he said. "Because it so happens that I love you, too."

And then he kissed her.

And as he was kissing her, he steered her toward the couch, swearing against her lips when he banged his shin on the coffee table.

Penny giggled.

Jason pulled back and looked around. "There really isn't a lot of room for two rug rats to run around here."

"I'm sure they'll manage."

He considered that for a minute. "And there's no backyard."

"We'll visit Uncle Travis's ranch to give them a real taste of the outdoors," she suggested.

"That's another thing."

"What is?"

"We're quite a distance from grandparents and aunts

and uncles who might otherwise be talked into babysitting every once in a while."

"Is there a point to all of this, or are you just thinking out loud?"

"I'm thinking that we need more space," he said again. "Yeah, maybe we could manage here with the twins, but what happens when we have another baby?"

"Another baby?"

"Or two."

"Could we get through *this* pregnancy first?"

"Of course," he agreed. "I'm just suggesting that we might want to rethink our living arrangements."

"You want to move?"

"Not right away. After all, it will take a while to decide on a plan, then find a builder, not to mention the time line for the actual construction."

"You want to *build* a house?"

He shrugged. "I figure, now that we've got a solid foundation, we can start building our future. And I want a house with a wide porch, where we can sit together when we're old and gray, and reminisce about where each of our children took his or her first steps. What do you think?"

He glanced down at her, saw that her eyes were all misty and soft. "I think it sounds wonderful."

"Good," he said. "Because I got a really good deal on some vacant land just outside of Dallas."

"But you work in Houston."

"Foley Industries has offices in Dallas, too," he reminded her.

"But what about your assistant? You always said you couldn't manage without her."

"Well, her husband is retired now, and, as it turns out, Dallas is actually closer to her new granddaughter, so Barb is quite happy to make the transition whenever we do."

"Is that really what *you* want?"

"I really want to be with you, and I can do that in Dallas as easily as anywhere else," he said.

"Speaking of which, we have to be there for dinner in less than six hours, so we'd better start getting ready, if we don't want to be late."

Jason tugged on the belt of her robe and the knot came undone. "Who says we don't want to be late?"

They made it on time…barely.

Of course, everyone else was already there when Jason and Penny arrived at the McCords' Dallas mansion. The house had been decorated to the nines, as it was for every holiday, but this year there was something extra—love was in the air, as tangible as the scent of pine and as intoxicating as the wine that was being poured at the table.

It had been a busy year for both families, and though there had been some trials and tribulations, everyone was looking forward to continuing to build the new relationships they'd established and to strengthen the bonds between the families.

"Grandma Eleanor," Olivia said, fairly bouncing up and down in her seat at the table. "I have something to tell you."

"What is it, sweetie?"

"You're going to be a grandma again."

"That's true," Eleanor said. "Because Auntie Penny's going to have a baby in June."

"And my new mommy's going to have a baby, too," the little girl proclaimed.

Unlike when Jason had announced Penny's pregnancy exactly one month earlier, the response to Zane and Melanie's news was overwhelmingly positive.

"And before you say anything, Dad," Zane announced, "yes, we are planning to get married."

"And definitely before the baby comes," Melanie assured everyone.

"Speaking of weddings," Eleanor said, shifting her attention to Tate and Tanya. "I just want to express our pleasure and gratitude that you were able to be here to celebrate with us today, despite your wedding being only a week away."

"Christmas is about family," Tanya said easily. "And I'm thrilled to be joining this one."

"And how are plans for your wedding coming?" Paige asked Katie.

"I've learned that a wedding is like a snowball," the bride-to-be responded. "The more you try to keep things rolling, the bigger and more unwieldy it seems to get."

"You wanted the big, formal wedding," Blake reminded her. "I just wanted to make you happy."

And it was obvious that they were.

"I have an announcement to make, too," Charlie said. "No, I'm not getting married or going to be a father," he hastened to assure them. "But it has to do with my father." He looked toward the head of the table, where Rex was seated, where Devon—the man he'd always believed was his father—used to preside. "I've decided to legally change my name to Charles McCord Foley."

Rex's hand shook slightly as he put his glass down,

and his eyes shimmered with an unfamiliar moisture. "Is this really what you want to do?"

"Yes, it's really what I want, so long as it's okay with you." He paused. "Dad."

Eleanor didn't try to hide the tears that spilled onto her cheeks.

"It's more than okay," Rex said gruffly. "It's the best Christmas present you could give me."

Olivia, bless her, lightened the moment by announcing, "I'd rather have a puppy."

Everyone laughed, but her father shook his head firmly. "You already have a kitten, and you have a baby brother or sister on the way, definitely no puppy."

As she pouted, Jason leaned closer to whisper in his wife's ear.

"I'll bet you she has a puppy before she has the baby brother or sister."

Penny shook her head. She'd seen, firsthand, how easily the little girl wrapped her daddy around her finger. "I'm not taking that bet."

Eleanor wiped her cheeks with her napkin, then lifted her glass. "To the Foleys and the McCords—a merging and ever-growing family."

Penny lifted her glass of nonalcoholic wine. "It's growing even more than you realize."

Paige, somehow instinctively guessing what her sister was going to say before she made the announcement, gasped. "Really?"

Penny nodded.

"Really what?" Tanya demanded.

It was Jason who answered the question. "Penny and I are expecting twin boys in early April."

"Twins?"

"Boys?"

"I think you're going to need a bigger place," Travis said.

Jason nodded. "We're hopefully going to start building early in the new year, not just because of the twins, but because I hope to have more babies with my incredible wife."

"Speaking of houses," Rex said, nudging his wife.

"I was going to wait until we were opening presents," she told him, but the excitement in her voice revealed her eagerness to share more news. "Since Travis has finally put a ring on Paige's finger—"

"I had to wait for my sister-in-law to create the perfect design," he told them, raising Paige's hand for everyone to see, then bringing it to his lips and brushing a kiss over her knuckles.

"As I was saying," Eleanor continued, "since the engagement is now official, I wanted to give you a special gift to commemorate the occasion."

But it was Paige who held up the envelope that had been hidden beneath her plate.

Travis's smile was quizzical as he lifted the flap and pulled out the folded papers. His eyes grew wide when he opened the document and realized what it was. His gaze went to Paige, who smiled and nodded, then to Eleanor, who also nodded.

"It's the deed to Travis's ranch," Paige announced to everyone, since her fiancé seemed too stunned to say anything.

"That's quite an engagement gift," he finally said.

"I wish I could say that I'd thought of it," Eleanor

said. "But it was Paige's idea. She thought it appropriate that the land you've worked for so long should finally be yours."

"Ours," he said, squeezing Paige's hand.

"Yours," she said, and leaned over to brush his lips with a quick kiss. "Until we're married, then it will be ours."

Everyone laughed.

Beneath the table, Jason linked his hand with Penny's.

She looked up and smiled at him, marveling at how much had changed in the four weeks that had passed since Thanksgiving. At that time, she'd been so hurt by Jason's deceptions and so filled with distrust, she didn't even know how to tell him that she was carrying his baby. Certainly she couldn't have imagined that, only a few weeks later, so much would have changed.

Now, there were no secrets between them and the promise of a beautiful future ahead.

* * * * *

Look for
THE ENGAGEMENT PROJECT
The first book in Brenda Harlen's new miniseries
for Silhouette Special Edition
BRIDES & BABIES
On sale January 2010,
wherever Silhouette Books are sold.

*Bestselling author Lynne Graham is back
with a fabulous new trilogy!*

PREGNANT BRIDES

Three ordinary girls—naive, but also honest and plucky…

*Three fabulously wealthy, impossibly handsome
and very ruthless men…*

*When opposites attract and passion leads to pregnancy…
it can only mean marriage!*

*Available next month from Harlequin Presents®:
the first installment*

DESERT PRINCE, BRIDE OF INNOCENCE

* * *

'THIS EVENING I'm flying to New York for two weeks,'
Jasim imparted with a casualness that made her heart sink
like a stone. 'That's why I had you brought here. I own this
apartment and you'll be comfortable here while I'm abroad.'

'I can afford my own accommodation although I may not
need it for long. I'll have another job by the time you
get back—'

Jasim released a slightly harsh laugh. 'There's no need for
you to look for another position. How would I ever see you?
Don't you understand what I'm offering you?'

Elinor stood very still. 'No, I must be incredibly thick
because I haven't quite worked out yet what you're offering
me.…'

His charismatic smile slashed his lean dark visage.
'Naturally, I want to take care of you.…'

HPEX0110A

'No, thanks.' Elinor forced a smile and mentally willed him not to demean her with some sordid proposition. 'The only man who will ever take *care* of me with my agreement will be my husband. I'm willing to wait for you to come back but I'm not willing to be kept by you. I'm a very independent woman and what I give, I give freely.'

Jasim frowned. 'You make it all sound so serious.'

'What happened between us last night left pure chaos in its wake. Right now, I don't know whether I'm on my head or my heels. I'll stay for a while because I have nowhere else to go in the short term. So maybe it's good that you'll be away for a while.'

Jasim pulled out his wallet to extract a card. 'My private number,' he told her, presenting her with it as though it was a precious gift, which indeed it was. Many women would have done just about anything to gain access to that direct hotline to him, but his staff guarded his privacy with scrupulous care.

Before he could close the wallet, his blood ran cold in his veins. How could he have made such a serious oversight? What if he had got her pregnant? He knew that an unplanned pregnancy would engulf his life like an avalanche, crush his freedom and suffocate him. He barely stilled a shudder at the threat of such an outcome and thought how ironic it was that what his older brother had longed and prayed for to secure the line to the throne should strike Jasim as an absolute disaster....

* * *

What will proud Prince Jasim do if Elinor is expecting his royal baby? Perhaps an arranged marriage is the only solution! But will Elinor agree? Find out in DESERT PRINCE, BRIDE OF INNOCENCE by Lynne Graham [#2884], available from Harlequin Presents® in January 2010.

Bestselling Harlequin Presents author

Lynne Graham

brings you an exciting new miniseries:

PREGNANT BRIDES

Inexperienced and expecting, they're forced to marry

Collect them all:

DESERT PRINCE, BRIDE OF INNOCENCE

January 2010

RUTHLESS MAGNATE, CONVENIENT WIFE

February 2010

GREEK TYCOON, INEXPERIENCED MISTRESS

March 2010

REQUEST YOUR FREE BOOKS!

2 FREE NOVELS PLUS 2 FREE GIFTS!

▼ *Silhouette*®

SPECIAL EDITION®

Life, Love and Family!

YES! Please send me 2 FREE Silhouette Special Edition® novels and my 2 FREE gifts (gifts are worth about $10). After receiving them, if I don't wish to receive any more books, I can return the shipping statement marked "cancel." If I don't cancel, I will receive 6 brand-new novels every month and be billed just $4.24 per book in the U.S. or $4.99 per book in Canada. That's a savings of at least 15% off the cover price! It's quite a bargain! Shipping and handling is just 50¢ per book.* I understand that accepting the 2 free books and gifts places me under no obligation to buy anything. I can always return a shipment and cancel at any time. Even if I never buy another book from Silhouette, the two free books and gifts are mine to keep forever.

235 SDN EYN4   335 SDN EYPG

Name	(PLEASE PRINT)

Address		Apt. #

City	State/Prov.	Zip/Postal Code

Signature (if under 18, a parent or guardian must sign)

Mail to the **Silhouette Reader Service:**
IN U.S.A.: P.O. Box 1867, Buffalo, NY 14240-1867
IN CANADA: P.O. Box 609, Fort Erie, Ontario L2A 5X3

Not valid to current subscribers of Silhouette Special Edition books.

Want to try two free books from another line?
Call 1-800-873-8635 or visit www.morefreebooks.com.

* Terms and prices subject to change without notice. Prices do not include applicable taxes. Sales tax applicable in N.Y. Canadian residents will be charged applicable provincial taxes and GST. Offer not valid in Quebec. This offer is limited to one order per household. All orders subject to approval. Credit or debit balances in a customer's account(s) may be offset by any other outstanding balance owed by or to the customer. Please allow 4 to 6 weeks for delivery. Offer available while quantities last.

Your Privacy: Silhouette is committed to protecting your privacy. Our Privacy Policy is available online at www.eHarlequin.com or upon request from the Reader Service. From time to time we make our lists of customers available to reputable third parties who may have a product or service of interest to you. If you would prefer we not share your name and address, please check here. ☐

SSE09R

Silhouette®

COMING NEXT MONTH
Available December 29, 2009

#2017 PRESCRIPTION FOR ROMANCE—Marie Ferrarella
The Baby Chase
Dr. Paul Armstrong had a funny feeling about Ramona Tate, the beautiful new PR manager for his famous fertility clinic. Was she a spy trying to uncover the institute's secrets…or a well-intentioned ingenue trying to steal his very heart?

#2018 BRANDED WITH HIS BABY—Stella Bagwell
Men of the West
Private nurse Maura Donovan had sworn off men—until she was trapped in close quarters during a freak thunderstorm with her patient's irresistible grandson Quint Cantrell. One thing led to another, and now she was pregnant with the rich rancher's baby!

#2019 LOVE AND THE SINGLE DAD—Susan Crosby
The McCoys of Chance City
On a rare visit to his hometown, photojournalist Donovan McCoy discovered he was the father of a young son. But the newly minted single dad wouldn't be single for long, if family law attorney—and former Chance City beauty queen—Laura Bannister had anything to say about it.

#2020 THE BACHELOR'S NORTHBRIDGE BRIDE—
Victoria Pade
Northbridge Nuptials
Prim redhead Kate Perry knew thrill seeker Ry Grayson spelled trouble. It was a case of the unstoppable bachelor colliding with the unmovable bachelorette. But did the undeniable attraction between them suggest there were some Northbridge Nuptials in their near future?

#2021 THE ENGAGEMENT PROJECT—Brenda Harlen
Brides & Babies
Gage Richmond was a love-'em-and-leave-'em type—until his CEO dad demanded he settle down or miss out on a promotion. Now it was time to see if beautiful research scientist Megan Rourke would pose as Gage's fake fiancée…and if their feelings would stay fake for long.

#2022 THE SHERIFF'S SECRET WIFE—Christyne Butler
Bartender Racy Dillon didn't expect to run into her hometown nemesis, Sheriff Gage Steele, in Vegas—let alone marry him in a moment of abandon! Now they were headed back to their small town with a big secret…but was there more to this whiplash wedding than met the eye?

SSECNMBPA1209

SPECIAL EDITION